The Fourth Island

ALSO BY SARAH TOLMIE

THE FOURTH ISLAND

SARAH TOLMIE

A TOM DOHERTY ASSOCIATES BOOK

NEW YORK

THE FOURTH ISLAND

Cover art by Rovina Cai
Cover design by Christine Foltzer

Edited by Carl Engle-Laird

A Tordotcom Book
Published by Tom Doherty Associates
120 Broadway
New York, NY 10271

www.tor.com

Tor® is a registered trademark of
Macmillan Publishing Group, LLC.

ISBN 978-1-250-76983-1 (ebook)
ISBN 978-1-250-76984-8 (trade paperback)

First Edition: October 2020

To L. Timmel Duchamp, with thanks

The man was not from the island. No one recognized him, though his face was well preserved. He had been in the water a while. There he lay, just as dead as any Conneely or Mullen or Derrane. But he was not a man of Inis Mór. Nor was he from the other Aran islands, the middle or the east. No. The women knew this. He lay face up. The pattern on the sweater was as clear as day and not one of them knew who had knitted it. They even brought out old Aoife, who had the sight-memory. She came hobbling out to the beach and fingered it with her swollen hands.

"Keep it," she said, "when you bury him. Get it off him. May come that we learn of it, but not if it's in the ground."

That made a scandal. To keep the things of a dead man, unburied or unburned. Bad luck, bad luck, may it be kept off. The men carried him into the village and asked Father Anselma. He said best to keep the body intact, as it was found; it was more seemly. Aoife said no and limped back to her fireside. There was a debate. Favour went with Aoife and not the priest. That happened sometimes.

"How you going to pray for him if you don't know

his name?" she asked. "No other way to learn it. It's writ there plain as plain if we find the woman who knit it."

"God knows his name," said Father Anselma.

"Bully for God," said Aoife.

They buried the stranger in consecrated ground, which was kind, as they hadn't much of it. The joke on the islands is that all men there are gods, as they've made the earth they walk on. From seaweed, sand, shit and time, on the face of the bare rock. *Fiat.* But it's not a joke for church. The stranger lay quiet in his plot, marked by a stone with a cross on it. From time to time, an unmarried woman, filled with sentiment, would lay a posy on it. Mary Mullen, in particular, was known to do this. She was a fine girl and it made the young men quite jealous. The dead have a pull to them.

No one wanted the dead man's sweater in the house. They had saved it but it was an uneasy object, not safe to keep. Aoife ended up keeping it. She was close to death anyway. Women came in ones and twos to talk it over. A few thought it looked O'Donnell, as if Tall Mary had made it, or one of her family on Inis Meáin. Some said maybe the Flahertys from the east island. Word went out to them over the months, as it always does. Fishermen's wives from the other islands even came to see it. Nobody claimed it. The funny thing was, though, everybody said it looked familiar.

The beautiful Mary Mullen came to see it. Two young men loitering over the net-mending saw her go in Aoife's door. No one with sense does that work outdoors when there's a fire inside. Yet a lot of men stood about outside with objects in their hands when Mary was out of a morning. Mary looked at the sweater thoughtfully. "It's like it comes from a family whose name I've just forgotten. Like long-lost relatives," she said.

"D'ye think if I put that damn sweater on, Mary'd recognize me as a long-lost relative? A relative of the marrying kind?" asked the younger Jim Conneely, plaintively. He spoke for many.

A bit of a war sprang up between Aoife and Father Anselma. Or a new skirmish in an old war. No one would expect the village wise woman, half a witch herself seemingly, and a learned man and a priest who had studied away on the continent for years and years to get on. People were none too certain that Aoife had ever been baptized. She was a law unto herself. And not, many respectable voices said, a good law. She was simply so old that the present generations in the town knew nothing about her origins, though there were many competing stories, none flattering. There had been a husband for a very short time—he who had built the cottage for her and cleared a field—but he had died. For all the years after, she had lived alone. The man was buried in the churchyard and she never visited his grave. She had little to do with the village, as a rule, except when people needed a cure. In that line, she was the authority for miles around. The money and gifts she earned for her remedies kept her in seed potatoes and kept her thatch mended. And in this way, of course, she also learned many of the town's secrets. People blab when they are ill. Women need certain cures. Men need other cures. She was the one who could provide them. Father Anselma might be the one who could mend souls, but she was the one who could mend bodies.

Aoife kept the dead man's sweater and women kept going to see it. Father Anselma considered this grotesque, verging on idolatry. "There are relics all over these islands, and that isn't one of them," he was known to say. He sensed a cabal forming. It made him uneasy. Aoife herself dismissed his opinion. She dismissed Father Anselma entirely. This fact caused the priest considerable pain, and he knew exactly why it was.

Eight years before, when he was newly arrived on Inis Mór, he, too, had fallen sick. In pain and trouble, he went to Aoife for a stomach remedy. She gave it to him. She was sly but civil. They briefly discussed his travels, and his reasons for coming to the island. He had made the terrible mistake of admitting to her that he had fled in the face of war. A hardness entered her eyes as he said this to her, and it never left. Father Anselma was ashamed. He upbraided himself for confessing such a thing to her. It had just been a moment of weakness because he had been feeling so poorly. But the damage was done. In a competition of shame, she would always have the upper hand of him. Shame is a vital weapon of priests. After all, they cannot use violence.

Moreover, Aoife had never passed a word of it on. No breath of rumour ever reached him from the parish. She might speak slightingly of him, but that was all. That was bearable. The upshot of it was that he owed her. She spared him, for her own reasons, whatever they were.

So, this war over the sweater and the impropriety of keeping it was a quiet one. It was confined to mutual sniping. But as it is with wars of this kind, people tended to take sides. Quietly. A certain coldness showed itself in the postures of some wives and mothers towards Father Anselma, even in church. Certain elders and men who considered themselves pillars of the community muttered more darkly than usual about Aoife and took care to be seen standing with Father Anselma on the church steps.

———————

Every village has its whore. In Cill Rónáin at that time

it was Nellie. Dirty Nellie. She was nobody's widow. She had never been married at all. She lived rough and was filthy, out in all weather. She never spoke. People didn't know if she was deaf or touched. She had run out of her parents' house when she was eleven. Soon after, they died. People said, of the shame. Some said, of the pox. However it was, she was alone after that. She would stay in no houses, but she would beg. People gave her enough to get by. She was one of their own.

Nellie took over Aoife's house when the old woman died. They found her in it when they went to burn it. The custom was to burn the thatch and all right down to the stone so it was clean. Then after a decent time, it might be rebuilt and somebody else live in the place, if it was a good one.

When they found her, Nellie was wearing the sweater. She stood silent in the doorway, defiant. The sweater hung down past her knees like a tunic. It was a man's garment.

A sudden rain came and put the torches out. People stood wondering what to do. Nobody wanted to touch her. Eventually they let her be. They crossed themselves and went home. Father Anselma thought about objecting. Part of him wanted to see the old woman's house burn, as an end to her recalcitrance. Then what the villagers considered a sanitary measure might also be the cremation of his secret shame. At the same time, he found himself disapproving of pisreogs such as this, which smacked of paganism. Fire made him nervous. People changed when fires were lit. He stood in silent debate with himself, looking at Nellie. It came to him that the cult of the sweater was at an end: no women would be coming to examine it now. Women had nothing to do with Nellie if they could help it. The charm was broken. He left with the crowd.

So after that, Nellie lived there, in Aoife's house. It never became her house. It was always Aoife's house. That's always what a man would say who went there to visit Nellie, if he said anything. That he was going to Aoife's house. Nellie lived there like she lived in a cave. She lit no fires. She did not mend the thatch. After dark, it was dark. She had no fuel or candles.

It was a matter of speculation in the village, whether or not she wore the dead man's sweater when she was with men, but none of them would ever say.

———————

And then suddenly, the sweater was gone, and Nellie with it. Nobody saw her go. Not on either road out of the village. Not over the fields. You could never sneak away over the fields, as you were forever climbing walls and could be seen for miles. She wasn't seen on the beaches, and no body washed up. Nellie had always shunned the sea. She wouldn't go near it even for shellfish.

Yet she was gone. So, the men had to do whatever with whatever urges they had, and the stranger's sweater and whatever it had said about the lost man's mysterious kinfolk were out of reach of the women, seemingly forever. Not but it had lost somewhat of its lustre latterly in belonging to Nellie. Except that it turned out, fortunately, that the youngest O'Donnell girl of the village, Mairín, who also had the sight-memory, had seen it. She could trace the pattern of it out, every cable and circle and triangle perfect as it was, with a burnt stick, or in a patch of wet sand. And this was very valuable in after days. It might even be safe to say that it saved Cill Rónáin, if not all of Inis Mór.

They burned the thatch of Aoife's house that had been Nellie's. It remained roofless for many years.

Life on Inis Mór has always been hard. Nobody moves to a windswept ledge of limestone at the farthest western edge of Europe, practically in the open Atlantic, for convenience. Irish people in modernity have been driven there by a series of brutal conquests of the mainland. Exactly why they lived there in the Bronze Age and Iron Age is a matter for conjecture. It is true that an island is easy to defend. Citizens of decadent Europe, of course, would question what there is in such a place that's worth defending.

First off, there is the ground. People throughout history and prehistory have defended the ground they live on. Hunter-gatherers protected their hunting grounds. Agriculturists protect their farmland, and they pour their desperate efforts into improving it with irrigation, fertilizer, crop rotation. Few of them, however, have had to make it. Earth. It is superabundant in other places. On the Aran isles, what little topsoil there is—a few inches at most—has been created by the men who farm it. Almost every spadeful of earth on Inis Mór—like Inis Meáin and Inis Oírr—was carried to its resting place by a man or a woman as a combination of sand and seaweed, with some fish and animal dung for good measure. They carried it inland from the ocean with barrows and spades and pitchforks and creels and their bare hands. They cut black weed and red weed and dozens of other weeds from the rocks with stone tools, bronze tools, then iron and steel tools. They carried thousands of pounds of sand and washed-up wrack from the foreshores all round the island. And then they waited for it to rot. While they did this, many of them starved. The animals they had brought from the mainland waited for grass. It is almost impossible to conceive how marginal it all was. Every pinch of soil on these islands is the product of human effort. The dirt is as precious as gold because it is an admixture of their hope and their despair.

Some eight months after the disappearance of Nellie, Jim Conneely the elder, him the uncle of the younger Jim Conneely who was known to hanker after the beautiful Mary Mullen, disappeared in his currach. This could not be said to be unusual, a man lost at the fishing, yet everyone felt that it was. Jim Conneely had been such a discontented man. People whispered that he had gone and killed himself, though they never said this in the hearing of the priest, and indeed the Conneelys had a most proper funeral for him after six months had gone by, though no body had turned up, not so much as a single pampootie. There was even a bit of a monument. Father Anselma said it was a *cenotaph*. That meant it was empty.

"Empty, right enough. Just like Jim," said the nephew. This was cruel, perhaps, but people agreed with him. The boy had admired his handsome uncle and namesake even though the man was always cold to him. Jim Conneely had been cold to everybody. He had been one of the best-looking men on the islands and had never made any good out of it. He left neither wife nor sons but many standing quarrels. At the time of his disappearance, he was twenty-seven years of age, well connected as to family, possessed land, boat and cattle, and had all his own teeth. He had absolutely no reason to be discontented. Yet he always had been. He was the kind of man who looked through people. Father Anselma was glad to be shot of him. He had not been a good Christian.

"He's off picking fights in heaven," said his sister Annie, not the only woman who had loved him with little encouragement, "Or sailing. He'd never go if there was no sailing." She laid flowers for him on his name day, on the empty monument, trying not to think where his pitiful body might be rotting and spinning now, lost.

———

Then they unexpectedly found it, the corpse of Jim Conneely. A full year after he'd left, fresh from the water, not more than two days dead. *Well, well,* some people said, *it's not more than you could expect if he'd run off to the mainland. Say he's been working away there all this time and then drowned and the waves brought him home. Could be that, like as not.* Why not? But it made them uneasy. One of the O'Donnells gazed down at the body and said, "Fetch

Mairín." He knelt down by Jim Conneely and looked hard at the sweater the man was wearing. To his eye it looked new. Rich wool, hardly worn. Made for him by some woman who loved him, and not one from Cill Rónáin.

"Do you recognize that?" he asked Mairín when she came, gesturing to the front panels of the sweater.

"Yes," replied the girl. She found a pointed rock and drew a pattern in the sand with her eyes closed. It was a party trick of hers. The man knew it. He compared it to Jim Conneely's fine sweater. The two were exactly the same.

"It's from the man in the graveyard," said Mairín.

"I thought so," he said.

So, that was something. What were they to do? Obviously, they ought to bury Conneely under his empty monument in the churchyard. That was the decent thing. But what of the foreign sweater? Should it go into the ground with him? They no longer had Aoife to advise. Wasn't it asking for trouble to leave a drowned man's garment unburied above the water line? They had kept the stranger's sweater in the village for a year and had never learned anything further about its origins. Aoife had died in the house with it. Nellie had disappeared with it. A dead man's garment is an ill-omened thing.

They buried Jim Conneely in his sweater with the unknown pattern. They held another funeral for good measure. At the same time, saying nothing about it to anybody, the O'Donnell who had found the body on the beach, Arthur O'Donnell, killed a calf. He scraped the hide and tanned it and prepared it and gave it to his cousin Mairín. She sketched out the pattern on it, the unknown one that seemed so curiously familiar, and he pricked it out and inked it. Then he rolled up the vellum and hid it away.

———————

Great stone-heavers, the people of the Aran islands. Enormous stone forts are here from truly ancient days. Ramparts and earthworks and fields of huge rocks set upright in the ground to break up armies. They rear up and bite the air, huge and scattered teeth torn from the jaws of a dragon, thrown down by local kings in the manner of Cadmus. These rocks speak of constant war. What did they have to defend, these Theban lords out at the edge of the world? Something. Something that they kept behind deep concentric walls and fathoms and furlongs and funnels of stone, stone and more stone. Petrified war.

So thought Father Anselma as he looked up at the ruins of Dún Aonghasa. He had got into the habit of making an annual pilgrimage to the heathen hill fort.

Not a proper, Christian pilgrimage. A pilgrimage of in-quiry. Or perhaps of resentment. A pilgrimage, howbeit, of some passion. He always went alone. The fact is, he was a bit of an antiquary. He had visited Roman ruins all over the Low Countries, musing on their significance. He had even been working on a book about them. Though the ruins out on these islands were not Roman. He didn't know what they were, except that they had been made by masters. Rulers.

From what titanic forces had these island chieftains sought to defend their wealth? The villagers of Cill Rónáin said, from the gods. The bad gods. Fomorians. Fir Bolc. No, thought Father Anselma, pacing around the monstrous walls. Nonsense. From other men.

A man who washes up on Inis Mór in a state as pristine as Jim Conneely can have hit the water no further off than Inis Oírr. He can't have come from the mainland either in Galway or Clare. It's too far and the seas are too rough. Or are we to believe he dropped from some monster ship out in the open ocean, heading for Amer-ica, say? Such a thing is not likely. And then, who but islanders wear these particular sweaters? Now, wherever there are sheep, there are women knitting sweaters. But the fact is, they are all different. They are different in the Hebrides. In the Orkneys and Shetland. Both the women and the sheep. No doubt they are different again in the big lands, all over, in Ireland and England and so on, whatever. The fact remains that any knitter in any town on any of the isles, or on any farm, knows a sweater knit here, in the Arans. She can probably tell you who knit it. She will know the wool and the stitches and the patterns common to each district and family and parish. She can probably tell you what saint's day it was finished on. And if she doesn't know herself, she knows a woman who will. Run to the end of that chain and whatever it is, there's no knowing it. So, when a woman tells you that this is undoubtedly an Aran sweater but that it was knit by a woman neither from Inis Mór nor Inis Meáin nor Inis Oírr, you are left with a riddle.

———

Now, Dirty Nellie understood many words but she didn't think in them. She watched the shapes of words on people's mouths and applied them to certain objects and situations, but in the main she got on quite well without them. A lot of what people said made no sense. Often they talked to pass the time, and time did not pass in that way for her. Generally, she preferred to be alone. After she had performed a certain act with Thomas Derrane at the age of thirteen or so, other men of the village began to come to her. She performed this act with them, too, using the parts of her body accommodated to such things. All other parts of her body had their uses. Legs for kicking and running and arms for swinging and hands for grabbing and so on. So, it seemed pretty straightforward. It wasn't always convenient but usually they brought food. Sometimes, they would share it with her, but more often, they left it. Sometimes, they brought clothing, cast-offs from their mothers and sisters. Or maybe they stole it. She once had a man's angry wife snatch a warm cap off her head as she passed through the village. After that, she always wore anything she was given that way far down inside any other clothes she was wearing so it couldn't be seen. It was safer.

She knew few women and liked none of them except for old Aoife. She begged in front of the houses of some of them when she had to. She did this by standing, or sometimes kneeling, with her hands clasped, within sight of their front windows, usually on a Sunday after church. Sometimes, she did this for a long time. But almost always, the woman of the house would come out and give her eggs or bread or some cooked meat or fish. Most of her winter clothing came to her in this way also. But she still did not trust them. Only old Aoife, who never gave her anything but allowed her to sleep by the hearth whenever she wanted, which she did quite often in winter. She would share her kills—hares, pheasants, mice—with Aoife sometimes and never stole her fowls. Any other chicken or duck she would kill if she found it unsupervised, but this was rare.

For a woman who lived on a small island, she spent very little time by the sea. She hated and feared it. She hated its constant, unpredictable motion. It was always leaping and creeping up on her. She could never take her eyes off it and this was very tiring. She noticed that others spent time by the sea and got food from its margins—seaweed, shelled creatures from the rocks—but she never tried, not even when she was starving. She was afraid of the ocean's endlessly reaching silent hands that would seize and drown her. Other people had some other resource, that sense that they all shared, the one that made the movements of their mouths meaningful to them, that offered them some protection from the sea. All those people who knew when a dog barked away behind them, they were safe. On land, she could tell when a dog, or a man, or another animal came near or went away. She could smell it. She could feel it in the ground. But the vile sea is always thrashing and its stink is constant. She kept right away from it.

This was her life until the pain began. Aoife thought

that she might be with child. The pain came from deep inside her. But she did not grow and though the pains went on for months, no child came. Aoife fed her many smelly herbs. Sometimes, the pain would stop for a while but never for long. By the time of the old woman's death, she was in constant agony. She wept and wept over the still body of Aoife by the hearth because the old woman was gone and she had loved her, and because she herself, Nellie, was still there. Death looked so restful.

After Aoife died, meaning no disrespect, she took the fisherman's sweater that the old woman had cherished. It was precious and many women had come to talk to Aoife about it. What they talked about on these occasions, Aoife had never been able to make clear to her. A number of words that she had never seen on the mouths of anyone were involved. Aoife would get excited trying to explain it. Her eyes would glisten. In the end, though, what Nellie knew was only that the sweater was different. It did not come from the village.

Nellie did not care. The fine, heavy wool was warm. The heat it made on her body dulled the pain. She stood up in it at Aoife's door and faced down the villagers when they came, all the angry women, even the priest. They went away, leaving the cottage unburnt. By then, Nellie herself was burning, burning and shivering by turns. The sweater became her only solace. She lay in it, hour after hour, not eating, not drinking, not sleeping, just being in pain. Pain is widely spoken of but it is impossible to convey how terrible it is. The sensation of the wool on her skin, its smell, its heat, its scratchiness, became the only things she had, other than the pain. Those things, and the pattern on the front panels. It lay over her chest and belly and groin, and she looked down at it constantly, like reading a book upside-down. Nellie could not read but she had seen Father Anselma's Bible. She had even held it in her hands for a blessing once when she was a young child. The priest had come and he and her parents, who never agreed about anything, had prayed fervently together. He never came again. Yet Nellie remembered this about the letters in a book: they looked sharply different upside-down or right-side-up. She thought of this, or felt this, as her fingers traced out the pattern again and again: the ball, the rope, the grass, the cow's hoof. How she was herself a book now, a white page. She saw the markings on the page one way; anyone looking at her would see it another. Which was right? The ball, the rope, the grass, the cow's hoof: the cow's hoof, the grass, the rope, the ball. Pain spread throughout her. It was her. Pain beheld her with another face. The ball, the rope, the grass, the cow's hoof; the hoof, the grass, the rope . . .

The door.

Jim Conneely ran aground on an island that wasn't there. Due north of Inis Mór, as far as he could reckon. When he spun around, confused, on the strand, he could see the north shore. Conneely was an impossible man and he had found an impossible island. *Well, isn't that just the way, now?* he thought, and shrugged, and sighed.

Seconds before, he had despaired of his life. There had been a squall. His currach had been carried rapidly towards the mouth of the bay. Much as he struggled against it, his tiny boat was rushing towards the open sea. His bones would wash up, years from now, on the coast of Newfoundland. It was all over. Of course, he had furled his wee sail at the first gusts of unmanageable wind. The monstrous idiocy of having a sail in a boat as small as this had struck him forcibly. He had bailed and bailed with his soft skin bag, the only thing you can bail a currach with without breaking its fragile skin. He had given up trying to impose any will on the thing at all. The tiny fat boat swung round and round on the waves in a final, fatal reel with the sea. Jim Conneely hated dancing. It was one of those innumerable things people did to pass the time that made no sense to him at all. To die this way was infuriating, but, clearly, die he must. Praying was out of the question. When had it ever done him, or anybody, any good at all? At the same time, there was no way he was resigned. Resignation was not for Jim Conneely. It was a pointless state of being. To resign meant to give something up in favour of something else, or at the will of someone else. To be resigned was always to be resigned *to*. He refused flatly to be resigned to anything or anybody. God. Death. None of it had anything to do with him. He was his own master.

The one thing he had never been able to master was the strange art of being Jim Conneely. But that was the challenge, though, wasn't it? Otherwise, he was one of those talented men to whom everything came easily. So, he had spent a lot of his time making things difficult for himself. The problem in this life, he thought, as the boat whirled sickeningly faster and faster as if on a potter's wheel, is that nobody ever leaves you *alone*. It just seems incredible to them that you don't want to master them, or be mastered by them, or whatever it is, that you might just want to confine yourself to governing what went on in your own head. Half the time, his head felt like a creel too full of fish, and wasn't it like that for everybody?

So, his thoughts spun on and on. The boat spun on and on. It was ridiculous. He could fill a whole prayer book with his thoughts from just these few minutes. You'd think he'd be a bit busier when dying. His mind was just readying itself to go off on some other tangent when, right through the skin of the boat, he felt land under his foot in its thin pampootie. And that was impossible, as he'd been lost in deep ocean a second before. The boat bobbed and stopped whirling. He was in that situation that it is only possible to be in while in a currach, that of being on land and water at the same time. He felt rock under his feet stretched out before him while his buttocks bounced lightly on rolling waves. A currach is a mad sort of boat. He was a mad sort of man. There was nothing to do but get out of the boat. So he did.

————————

Every person who has ever lived in Ireland has heard of Oliver Cromwell. Even the gods have heard of him by now. Insofar as the Arans are part of Ireland, always a matter for debate—for either they are islands entire of themselves, or they are the quintessence of Irishness, unless perhaps the two are the same—the people here, too, retain a deep and scarred memory of that terrible man. He and his army crossed Inis Mór in 1650. He incarcerated many priests on Inis Oírr, and you can still hear their ghostly orisons when the wind is easterly. So, it will surprise nobody that Cromwell left his mark even on Inis Caillte, the fourth Aran island, the lost one.

Thus, the first person that Jim Conneely met on Inis

Caillte was a camp follower from Cromwell's army. Of all kinds of human being that it is possible to be, a Cromwellian camp follower is one of the worst. Sex and Puritanism are hard companions. The Wars of the Three Kingdoms were hard on all of the men in all of the armies, but let it be said now that they were even harder on the women. It must be reckoned to Jim Conneely's credit that he perceived this almost at once.

The first that he noticed of Meg Haylock was her scarred hand on his gunwale, pulling the currach gingerly in to shore. She had been cut by a sword and was missing her little finger. When he looked up at her face, he saw it was heavily scarred by what he thought must have been the pox, though it turned out to be the bubonic plague.

"Hup," she said to him with a quick jerk of her head, indicating the rocky beach. He hopped out of the boat and collapsed as his frozen knees gave way. He crawled forward and helped her heave the currach gently over the rocks. It was so astonishing that the hide wasn't ripped to shreds already that it seemed a shame to tear it now. The two of them got the little craft above the water line.

"Who are you?" he asked when he got his breath back.

"Meg Haylock," she said. Her voice was deep and burry.

"Where do you come from?"

"Huntingdon."

"And where's that?"

"Near Cambridge."

"You don't mean to tell me that this is England?"

"No," said Meg, "this isn't England." As it happens, she was speaking English, a language that Jim did not know. He only worked that out later. But the first rule is that all of the lost can understand each other. It's an admirable rule.

"How did you end up here? Do you know?" asked Jim.

"One minute, I was being crushed into the mud by fleeing men, and then I was here," replied Meg.

"And how did you feel?" asked Jim, as this seemed important.

"Then? Sick. And angry. Scared. After that, just surprised. I've been surprised ever since I got here."

"And when was that?"

"I don't rightly know. I should say maybe a couple of months. My wounds healed."

"You said men were fleeing? Was there an army? What army?"

"The army of the Parliament. Ironsides. I was with my brother, and his friend, my betrothed before he died. They were infantry. I started out a washerwoman."

"I ought to kill you," said Jim Conneely.

"I don't know that it works that way here," said Meg.

"What, we're in heaven, then, are we?" said Jim, acidly.

"There's no such thing as heaven," replied Meg.

"Well, that's one thing we can agree on, anyway," said Jim.

When Nellie arrived on Inis Caillte through the blazing door of her own pain, the first thing she met was the sea. Nor was she pleased to do so. She lay on a patch of damp grass close to a rocky shore. While her insides were no longer burning, she was instantly and thoroughly uncomfortable. All around her, and going right through her head like a knife, was a great whooshing, thundering roar. It was horrible and vast and got right inside her. She sat up. The grass stems made a kind of squeaking rustle. They seemed alive. It was terrible. She shrank away from them. The rushing and sighing of the air by her ears, in her ears, went on and on. A cricket hopped and made a nasty clicking noise. Noise. That's what it all was. Of course, it's completely stupid to describe it in this way, as Nellie did not have words for *roar, rustle, click* or *noise*. She could not match them with any sensations. But this was trivia. Much worse was that she could not match the sensations she was now having, which were those of hearing, with the ones she was used to. With seeing and feeling and smelling and understanding where her limbs were in space. Hearing, if you must do it for the first time, is positively deafening. After five more minutes of it, she had to roll over and vomit. She sat trembling for fifteen more minutes before she could get up or move around. When she did, she got dreadful vertigo every time she looked at the sea beating and beating against the shore. It called attention to itself like a crying baby or a needy drunk, endlessly. She shaped her lips into a word she had seen on Aoife's mouth, and others.' *Loud*.

Fortunately, she breathed it only and made no sound. She was spared the further shock of listening to her own voice, as untrained as that of a wild animal.

So, Nellie was unusual in that the first human voice she heard was not her own.

The second person Jim Conneely met on Inis Caillte was Mary MacIntosh, the girl he was going to marry. He wouldn't have called himself a marrying man at the time.

He and Meg Haylock were proceeding inland across a field of sheep, quite companionably. Jim felt on the one hand that he was in duty bound to throttle her as an enemy of his people, and on the other an equally strong resistance to doing anything that duty bound him to do. As Meg was big and strong and pretty well as tall as he was, and quite unperturbed by their uncanny situation, he figured that the sensible thing was to go along with her in case he needed an ally. She had helped him out with the currach.

There was an uncommonly pretty girl watching over the sheep. "Ah, Mary," said Meg, coming up to her, "Look, here's another one. His name is Jim."

"Jim Conneely," he said, and wished he had a cap to remove with a flourish. Unfortunately, his cap had been the first victim of the squall that had brought him there. There was no cap in history that would have made it through such a gale, not even one belonging to Hannibal.

"Are you a Conneely from Inis Mór, then?" said the pretty girl, Mary.

Jim was thunderstruck. "Yes!" he said. "Yes, I am! It seems to me that it's just over there, no more than a mile south. Is that true? How can that be?" And then he added, "And you, Miss MacIntosh, are you from around here?"

"It's true it's no more than mile. Still, it's very hard to get to. Half the time, we can't even see it. And I myself"—she smiled gaily, showing a dimple on one side—"am a native of this place, Inis Caillte. These are my father's sheep. Our farm is just over the hill."

"So, there are people from here, born here?" asked Jim, eagerly. "It's not just that lost people wash up here?"

"Oh, no," said Mary, "It's the whole island that's lost. We've been on it a long time. As long as you on the other islands, I expect. You know how it is on an island. We're independent. But there's something about this island that attracts the lost. Like a lodestone. They're drawn here. They pop up from time to time."

"From anywhere?"

"So it would seem. My father once met an Afric prince."

"But Meg here is from the from the seventeenth century! From the time of the Cromwellian wars! That's two hundred years ago! And she's been here only a few months."

"Yes," said Mary, "it works like that."

"What year is it, anno domini? Here?"

"1840," said Mary. "Why, what is it where you come from?"

"1840," said Jim, relieved. He didn't want to live through the Middle Ages. "How's the fishing?" he said.

———————

Meg Haylock came from the same village as Cromwell himself, the great general. The Lord Protector. She and her brother got some credit for this. Cromwell had been their member of Parliament, though of course their family were not of the class who could vote. They were good Puritans, though, dissatisfied with Anglican compromise and with a healthy hatred for the foreign and Catholic-loving king. There had been a party with a bonfire in Huntingdon at the news of Charles's execution. Ah, the Parliament was bringing a new day!

Of course, this new day couldn't dawn until they had mopped up the king's Catholic allies, many of whom were in Ireland, another foreign nation. And while the Haylocks, as yeomen, couldn't vote, they were perfectly acceptable to the Parliamentary army. Meg's brother joined and was given a pike and a helm and some plated leather armour and some infantry drill. And a wage. Meg joined too and was given none of these things. That is, she went along with her brother and his friend Christopher, to whom she had become engaged at the bonfire party, as they departed the fens, first for London and then for Dublin. Their parents were dead and their farm had been first mortgaged and then destroyed in the fighting that swirled over East Anglia in the early years of the civil wars. Even the New-Modelled Army needed women. Armies needed cooking and cleaning and carrying and comfort; everybody knew that. She wasn't the only local woman to go. None came back.

Christopher died of dysentery weeks after they landed. He never saw any action. For Meg, the main action of the war in Ireland was marching in mud, closely followed by fighting for space in wagons, lifting heavy objects, lighting fires in rain, and strapping wounds and ulcers in the feet of her brother and his immediate friends. Then she was raped by some ally or other, a Presbyterian—he had a Scots accent—on a field during the siege of Wexford. There was a lot of ferocity during that siege, and ferocity spreads in every direction. After that, her reputation was tarnished. Her brother couldn't protect her, and after a while, he didn't care to. Having a whore for a sister has many perks in a near-starving army. The wench from Huntingdon increased in value as the campaigns went on. It was as close as men could come to fucking Cromwell.

Meg took care of herself as best she could. She even took care of her brother, who was as trapped as she was. They walked clear across Ireland, getting sicker and angrier and dying by inches. There were a few battles, which were loud and confused; sieges, which meant waiting around and endless thieving; a few times they drove parties of prisoners before them. These prisoners were mostly poor, ragged men who spoke only Irish. Nobody could get sense out of them. Sometimes they prayed, or sang. The army resented them: they were not worth feeding. Often, they let them escape for that reason. Some were rescued by locals who raided by night, always lead-ing to losses. Prisoners were a bad business. No regiment wanted them. There were fewer of them as they went west. Meg did see people fleeing, though. Families, women, even a priest or two, carrying as much as they could on their backs. God knows where they were going. Into the sea, perhaps. The Parliamentarians let them go, only taking their bacon or fowls, though occasionally they killed the priests. They knew the priests would not recant, and they were at war with the Roman church, weren't they?

Meg and her brother and the last few men she knew from Huntingdon, plus some eight hundred men or so, made it as far as some nameless moor in Connacht. There they definitely lost a battle against a group of well-armed and organized Irishmen under the command of a local lord, who had some horses left. Most of the men had cut down their pikes long since to make them easier to carry. They were used to fighting men on foot. A shorter pike is fine for that. But you need the length to turn horses. The Englishmen lost. Horses and men over-ran them, and those who could still flee ran for it. Meg, in a field behind the front where the men had been lined up, had the battle fall back and run straight over her. She and the other remaining women, the cripples and camp fol-lowers and baggage-carriers, were suddenly in the middle of a crowd of men screaming in Irish and English. There was running. There were pounding hooves, foundering and falling bodies. Within minutes, Meg herself fell. She held up her hand to ward her face and a sword sliced off her finger. Then she was gone.

Nobody missed her because they were all dead. But when Meg came to, on the damp grass that she assumed was endemic to Ireland, she was on Inis Caillte.

Wandering around a day later, weak from loss of blood and beginning to be feverish, she met Mary MacIntosh, out watching over the sheep. Mary was kind to Meg, even after she learned she was English, and Meg was astonished to find that she understood her. She had never understood an Irish speaker before. Meg was led back to the MacIntosh farm and looked after while her hand healed. The family didn't even shun her when they learned she had travelled with the Ironsides.

"There's no call for those old enmities here," said Conor MacIntosh, Mary's uncle. "They're not very real to us as was born here," he went on, "seeing as we only seem to connect to the other islands, let alone the mainland, from time to time. Dipping into certain chapters of a long book, like, and skipping the rest? And then, the people who comes to us, we've found over the years that they're all equally lost. It's hard to be loster'n somebody else. It's even-steven."

The family was, however, extremely interested in

Oliver Cromwell. Once they understood that she had crossed the country with his army, they were full of questions about him. Was he, in fact, a giant, a sort of blood-soaked ogre? Did he kill priests and women with his bare hands? How many people really had died after his army took Drogheda? Did he believe in God?

"I never met him," said Meg, "Nor did my brother. But he did come from our borough. Huntingdon. I think he was gone from Ireland before our regiment fell. He went back to be Lord Protector and run the government with the rest of the Parliament, I expect. I don't know what happened to him."

"He died," said Mary, "And then the king came back."

"What, Charles the Scot? He was dead!" said Meg.

"No, his son, I heard. I think his name was Charles too, though."

"That's terrible," said Meg, "So, are there still kings and dynasties in England now, then?"

"Yes," said Conor, nodding, "There's a queen, Victoria. From Hanover. She's even queen of Ireland, people say."

"Isn't that in Germany, Hanover?" asked Meg.

"Yes."

"And she's queen of England?" said Meg, "Is she a Protestant—a Lutheran, or what?"

"All I know is she's not a Catholic," said Mary. "Philip Murphy was very clear about that."

"And who's he?"

"A Catholic priest. He arrived not long before you did. From the Low Countries, he said. There was a war," replied Mary.

"There's always a war," said Meg.

———————

Jim had been living on Inis Caillte and cosying up to Mary MacIntosh for two months, working for her father as a herdsman and fisherman by turns. MacIntosh was glad of the help, as he had a lame leg. There was nothing else Jim could do, as he was not a landholder there. Not but there was a lot of free land, and quite fertile, too.

So, for the first time, he had gone on an expedition. He decided to look at the northwest of the country. He was always the man looking for land's end and the open sea. There he was, on a headland, gazing out at what must surely still be the mouth of Galway Bay and wondering if he sailed out there, would he end up in some imaginary America, when somebody pulled on his sleeve.

He turned and saw a small, fine-boned woman with black eyes and a fountain of heavy black hair.

"Jim Conneely?" she said, in the toneless voice of a sleepwalker.

He had not the slightest idea who she was.

"I am Nellie," she said, "of Cill Rónáin. She who was dumb."

"Nellie!" he returned in amazement. He had not been one of her patrons but knew several men who had been.

"Dirty Nellie," she said in her light voice, and looked at him.

"No longer dirty, I see. As clean as a well bucket," he said gallantly, wincing at his comparison. He pressed on, "And dumb no more. Was it one of the miracles of this place?"

She looked at him steadily.

The gallantry had been a mistake. It was not his custom to treat woman like fools. Formerly, he had tried to avoid them altogether. But between his courtship of Mary and what he would have to describe as the beginning of a friendship with Meg Haylock, the situation was now somewhat different.

"So, that was stupid, wasn't it? Whatever it is that goes on here doesn't strike me a miraculous. Unless you count the fact that I've met only the one priest on an island this size. I'd describe it more as a freak of nature," said Jim.

"There are two priests," said Nellie, smiling.

"No miracles, then," said Jim. "Can I ask you how you came to be here? Do you remember it?"

"Pain," replied Nellie. "I just thought I'd died. But I

woke up on the shore here."

"How is it that you speak so well now?"

"I married a man," said Nellie, "A learned man. A priest."

"A priest!" yelped Jim. Then he paused, embarrassed at his own shock. Was he a grown man, or a child? "So, he's a priest no longer, then? He gave it up?"

"He's still a priest," said Nellie.

"Is he a Protestant man?"

"No," said Nellie.

"It's beyond me, then," said Jim, firmly.

"Yes," said Nellie.

Jim was amazed at her assurance. But then, he thought, if whatever had happened to her on this island was as odd as had happened to him, there wasn't much point in clinging to the old certainties. "But he's not from Inis Mór, your husband, is he?" he asked.

"No, he's from the mainland. The funny thing is, he knew Father Anselma. They met in Brussels, in seminary there. He got caught up in politics in '30. So did Father Anselma, he says, though he had a different name then."

"Bad politics?" said Jim.

"Bad," nodded Nellie.

This was the last conversation he could have imagined himself having with Dirty Nellie, the village whore. Not that he could have had a conversation with her at all in

Cill Rónáin. He thought of his conversations with Meg, who spoke no Irish. It came to him in a kind of grim flash that the deaf and illiterate girl from his own village had been as lost to him as an English woman from the seventeenth century. For that was what this was, the lost speaking to each other. It made him want to sit down and reckon up the ways in which he himself was lost, and even—the thought made him uncomfortable—to whom.

He walked back with Nellie to a very pleasant cottage in a glen and met her husband, Philip Murphy from County Clare. He was a slight, quick-witted, talkative man with brown hair and a long nose, and he and Nellie seemed most domestic. He had three books in his house, from which he had taught Nellie to read. "I chanced to have them with me when I met the bayonet that brought me here," he said, but did not elaborate. Philip spoke Irish, but a number of other languages, too. For the sake of simplicity, Jim assumed that they all spoke Irish together—he heard it as Irish—but he couldn't be sure. He heard Irish when Meg spoke, as well.

"There's good land around here," remarked Jim, "Do you know who owns it? Do you?"

"I feel I own the cottage. I helped to build it. The land, I don't know. I farm a little of it, though God knows I'm no great farmer," said Philip. "No one else lives too close."

"I might claim some of it, a ways off, if you've no objection," said Jim, "I've a mind to get married as soon as possible. Though it seems an odd way of going about it. I'll never know if it's mine or not."

"It's not like you owned your land at home," said Philip, with a gleam in his eye.

"Didn't I?" said Jim.

"No," said Philip, "Not in the law, you didn't. It's a sin and a crime, but you never did, as you well know."

"I've never met a radical priest," Jim couldn't help saying.

"Well, you have now," said Philip.

Jim walked slowly home to the MacIntosh farm, thinking of Philip Murphy. If you lose, are you lost? He asked Mary to marry him and she said yes.

So. That's how it came that Jim Conneely was found washed up on Inis Mór in a sweater that nobody knew but that was nonetheless an Aran sweater. His wife Mary of Inis Caillte knit it for him. The ball, the rope, the grass, the cow's hoof: the pattern that women on the MacIntosh farm had been knitting with the wool of their own sheep for generations. The death of Jim was a terrible thing. He was a new-married man with a pregnant wife and a cottage barely built. He was a man just learning to sleep soundly in his own skin. He went out in his currach to fish and he never came back.

The death of any person is a terrible thing. But the lost are as mortal as anyone.

———————

Now, you might be wanting to know a bit more about Inis Caillte. There's not a great deal that we do know. One is that the island has a lot more timber than the other islands. So, the cottages of Nellie and Philip, and of Mary and Jim, had a lot more wood in them than the stone cottages of Inis Mór or the western mainland. They went up the quicker for it, which is why Jim had a cottage all built before he died. He only helped the MacIntosh men to build it, as he wasn't accustomed to building in wood. He found that embarrassing, but the work got on fast for all that. Also, on Inis Caillte, there are no potatoes. Jim had been horrified at this.

"But you'll starve!" he said.

The fact is, on Inis Caillte they grew more grain. Not a great deal, so flour was precious. It was used a lot in barter, as a matter of fact. It was the island's own gold. The soil was deeper and richer near the trees, and by careful cultivation of small, irregular plots they could get good wheat, up to three crops a year. You'd think it might be a matter of stone querns and hand milling and all that nightmare after that, but as it happens, they had a windmill. Yes. It had been built by a Fleming in 1713. He had been on the wrong side of the War of the Spanish Succession. Sometimes, the lost are of great use to each other.

"But potatoes!" said Jim. He couldn't believe it. "There really aren't any here? Why not, I wonder?" he said to Mary.

"Well, you didn't have any on you when you landed, did you?" said Mary, reasonably, "And I guess nobody else did either. They're great heavy roots, you say? A pocket full of seed's a lot easier. And maybe they're more of a found thing than a lost thing. They're not from here, anyway." And that was that.

Jim missed potatoes. This surprised him, as he had hated them back home. The Jim Conneely of Cill Rónáin had been a fisherman who hated fish and a herdsman who hated cows and a farmer who hated potatoes. But Inis Caillte was softening him somehow. Heaven knows the man he might have become had he not drowned.

In other respects, the island was much like the other islands. The weather was temperate, the winds were high, and the people ate more seaweed than they do in other lands. However, there were no big towns, and no churches, and people lived scattered all over on farms and homesteads. It wasn't a very populous place. You'd have thought it would be, as there are an awful lot of the lost. But it wasn't.

———————

On Inis Mór, things went on much as they had before. Mairín O'Donnell was called on from time to time at this gathering or that to sketch out the mysterious panels from the unknown sweaters, and everybody would muse on them and make various suggestions. But gradually, the reappearance of Jim and the disappearance of Nellie moved to the back of people's minds and there they stayed.

Only Arthur O'Donnell, who had inked out the pattern on vellum, remained fascinated by it. As it was, in the end, a piece of knitting, it seemed a bit of a girlie fascination, so he didn't say much about it. But from time to time, he would draw it out of the chest where he kept it and pore over it a while. There was a round form he hadn't seen in knit patterns before. Knitters on Inis Mór didn't go in for circles. What was it? He assumed it was something. A hurley ball? A clochán seen from the top? The turd of a hare? A fish's roe? What else is round? There was a pair of triangles side by side like hills with a valley between them. Or maybe more like a rectangle with a triangular bite out of the top, like a notched bonnet ribbon. Or like the cloven hoof of a deer or a cow. And then there were cables and textured bits that he'd seen before, each of which was supposed to have a different meaning. He couldn't make any kind of sense out of it. Not that he'd ever got much meaning out of the sweater patterns people had explained to him, the ones supposedly associated with this or that name, or parish, or woman. They didn't tell stories. They were like the markings on flags or the emblems of noblemen: signs of a clan or a tribe. What could they really say, except maybe how people made their living? Well, he could see that a living could be made out of cows. Or cables, if they were fishermen's ropes. But he couldn't for the life of him think what living could be made out of a ball. Perhaps it was a basket—a creel, say? A buoy? Then it struck him that maybe it was the sun, like on old pagan things. But that wasn't much use. Everyone has an equal claim on the sun. It lights everybody. Why would you want that mixed up with your profession, or your family? It doesn't make much of a distinction. The moon? And the moon would mean what, then? Tides? The bleeds of women? Any number of foolish pisreogs?

He would get about this far down any mental track and become embarrassed with himself. Then he would roll the leather carefully back up and put it away. He would have felt better about it had it been a map. A map is a manly thing. But things woven out of wool ought to be women's business. We kill an animal and take its skin, or we crop its living hair like grass, and that makes all the difference.

———————

On Inis Caillte, Meg had stayed for some time with the MacIntoshes, and then, to her amazement, they helped to build her a cottage. It wasn't a very big one, just one room and a hearth, but it was hers. It may be said that she was a lot more useful in the building of hers than either Jim Conneely or Philip Murphy were in the building of theirs. For one thing, she had seen houses framed with timber before—there are plenty of trees in East Anglia—unlike Jim, and she was a much sturdier worker than Philip, who was vague and easily distracted.

"There's a woman with a lot of sense, now," said Conor MacIntosh. He was a widower and looked at Meg with a bit of a glad eye. She kept herself to herself, however, and showed no inclination to settle down with anyone. She did accept an ewe and a ram lamb from Conor, though. At first, she had suggested a very frank way for herself to earn the sheep from him. Conor was aghast but that's not to say he wasn't tempted. But he up and gave her the animals outright in the end. He examined his feelings and concluded that he was a marrying kind of man and that was the end of it. If Meg Haylock was not a marrying woman, so be it.

Meg started a kitchen garden. She walled it to keep

out the sheep. Her ram lamb, Werther, was a feisty one. He leapt her walls continually, so she had to keep building them higher. She drafted in help from children and any other willing hands for miles around. Werther nearly killed himself trying to climb the walls when they got too tall to jump. Meg spent a goodly amount of time cleaning out wounds in his spindly legs. He was a determined cabbage fancier.

Jim Conneely helped her out a lot with the garden walls. He also showed her a few things about handling sheep. Meg had experience with poultry and cows—their farm in Huntington had had a dairy once—but not sheep. They were even stupider than she had expected. Werther was endearing, though. "Little idiot," said Jim one day, slinging the lamb across his back and carrying him out of the garden for the fourth time as the walls were building. "He could break his neck. Sheep are actually capable of dying of stupidity."

Meg laughed, but then she said, "So are men. I saw many do just that. It was horrible, really."

"In the war?' asked Jim, startled.

"There's nothing stupider than men at war," said Meg, "or nothing that I've seen, at least. Everybody's witless most of the time. Drunk or terrified. Sick half to death, or raving. Following orders that make no sense. Or giving them."

"Sure and that's not very dignified," said Jim, feeling affronted on behalf of his sex in their martial endeavours and then remembering that she was talking about Englishmen, for whose dignity he was not supposed to care.

"Dignity's the first thing to go on a campaign," said Meg, "what with people so jammed up together. Sleeping in tents and haystacks. Food always too hot or too cold and never anything to carry it in. Crowded latrines. Finding a peaceful place to take a shit was enough to thank God on."

"Not very heroic," said Jim.

"Not very," agreed Meg.

———

Nellie's disease, whatever it was that had caused her such killing pain, vanished on Inis Caillte. So did the disease of her deafness. She did not miss the one but often she missed the other. She had not thought of deafness as a disease, anyway. It was simply how she was, and correspondingly how the world was. Occasionally, she longed for that world again. The bellowing of cattle, the fierce sound of the wind at night, and, truth be told, the nattering of some of the Flaherty women, made her wish for the world of unhearing. That world is very vivid but it comes at you in different ways and at differing rates. She remembered it, overall, as slower. But it could be that it was the slowness of memory she recalled rather than slow experience. She remembered being able to watch things unfold with a tremendous attention—a beetle traversing a leaf, say—that she now found hard to recapture. The endless bath of sound was distracting. She wondered how people bore it. How, for example, had they been able to stand it when they were babies? Maybe that was why babies spent so much of their time crying. But then they had to listen to themselves cry, too. It was a puzzle.

The murderous pain she did not miss at all. But where had it gone? Would it ever come back? Once you have had pain like that, you dread its onslaught ever after. The fear of it never leaves you alone. Just as the pain itself once was, it becomes your constant companion. Nellie was haunted by that fear. So, it cannot be said that her transition to Inis Caillte was a transition to perfection. It was an improvement, a place of safety. That was also how it seemed to the other newcomers she talked to. The one thing she dwelt on was the loss of her deafness—it was a loss, the loss of the person she had been before—and its meaning. Meg and Jim and Philip had been saved from death, as she had been. Yet none of them had been changed to the extent that she had. They all talked about it.

"It seems to me it's akin to this ability we all have now

to understand each other's languages. I mean, God only knows what language it is that we're speaking now," said Philip.

Nellie agreed with him. "I believe you," she said. "But I have to tell you, I do feel a bit interfered with. If it's God who did this, he's a bossy fellow."

"God's got nothing to do with it," said Jim. Meg nodded. They were both cheerful atheists. But Philip was not, and Nellie was not sure what she was.

"We're miles off any scripture I know," admitted Philip, "or any prophecy or vision. Unless they're all a lot more metaphorical than I thought. But I'm just so accustomed to the idea of God running things—the world, you know, the universe—that I can't let go of it. I don't insist that any of you go along with me. I feel I've lost my foothold for insistence."

"You're a sly one, Father," said Jim, "being so nice about it but keeping God's card on the table. He's always been there to explain the mysterious things, and here we are in the midst of one—"

"But you could have said that before! About your life back home. Any of us could!" interrupted Philip.

"More slyness," said Jim, shortly. "We're not in heaven and we're not in hell. I don't think any of us died. We're here somehow, still living. The whole business isn't like any Christian promise I ever heard of, and it blows the whole idea out of the water."

"Purgatory?" said Philip.

Meg looked at Philip. "That's nonsensical popish superstition, Father."

"It is a bit old-fashioned," said Philip. "Besides, it seems selfish to suggest that this whole island exists just to test us, or to allow us to work off our sins."

"I don't know that I'd need so much ground for that," said Jim. "And what about the other people here? The Flahertys? Mary?"

"Has it occurred to you that in being a good husband to Mary, you might be answering for being the hard man that you were before?" said Philip.

"And Mary's just a prop, then, in my salvation, is she?" asked Jim.

"No, of course not," said Philip. "She's her own person with her own soul. But it does make me wonder how much we are all implicated in each other's salvation."

"You go on wondering, Father, and leave me and Mary out of it," responded Jim.

Meg and Nellie watched this exchange with impatience and indulgence, perhaps with a slyness of their own: the slyness of women observing the tiltyard men must make out of everything. Nellie felt that they had strayed a considerable distance from the topic of her deafness.

"Well, we might say, then, that we were all cured of

deafness, in suddenly understanding all these languages," said Nellie. "It wasn't that God just poked holes in my ears and let the world in. It happened to all of us."

Everyone blinked a few times and focused on Nellie. "Yes," said Philip. "Language is an instrument for revealing the world. The world of other people, at least. I guess we all needed more of that world. Maybe that's why we're here."

"And maybe it isn't," said Jim, "And we just need to let the world get on with the job, eh?"

———————

Now, there are no ruined hill forts or monasteries on Inis Caillte. It is a place of lost people but not lost things. Our world is the world of the lost things. It's the only way we know about the lost people. You can see that on the Lost Isle, there would be no need. The people are there. But not many of them.

Why would they not be there in their hundreds and thousands, in their millions? The lost? Now, let us hope that it is as many wise people have theorized: that they are there. Perhaps we just can't see them. We can't account for them. Not so many at a time. Would you want to be lost with three billion others, for example? Or just with a few? That story would be easier to tell. It would be cruel to suggest that there is a quota of the lost—let us say, only, that on Inis Caillte we are dealing with one of many, perhaps infinitely many, overlapping planes or interweaving tales. We are dealing with just so many as we can hold in our sympathies at one time. Those are the limits of the island. There are no others.

Father Anselma, who looked up at the huge broken fortress of Dún Aonghasa on Inis Mór with his heart full of rage against the overlords and hoarders and murdering usurpers of the earth, surely might have been counted as one of the lost. Authoritarian war had swept him right to the edge of the map of Europe. He thought he had left Ireland to help bring God's peace and the message of the poor to a radicalized continent, and he was driven straight back to Ireland to poorer people than ever. He died of typhoid in 1847 working among his starving parishioners. He was not a bad man. But he would never have gone to Inis Caillte.

Father Anselma considered it a miracle that he had once survived a riot in Brussels, a miracle that he did not deserve. The riot had been brutally put down by an army of the United Netherlands. Almost everybody around him had died. He had been there in good conscience, in what had begun as a peaceful protest against a heedless empire. Men had marched and carried signs in French and Flemish. He had marched among them, supporting his new parishioners. The archbishop had just granted him a tiny but populous parish near Aarschot. He had been very proud of himself, to get such a post even though he was a foreigner. Anselma had been a rising star at the seminary. When the Dutch had started shooting into the crowd, incredibly, amid the surge of desperate people, he had found a way out, dropping and crawling into a side street. In terror, he had walked and begged rides in farm wagons all the way to a distant port and got the first boat he could to England, and then on to Ireland. He had let his bishop think he was dead. He had abandoned his post. He had seen all those people dying and assumed that the cause of freedom was lost. He was lost. The independent kingdom of Belgium was founded the next year, and Anselma, hating himself, had nothing to do with it. He took vows as a Carmelite—and with them his new name—and determined to give his life meaning by serving in the remotest Irish parish he could find. He would never have traded that meaning for some kind of new start on a pagan island.

There are so many ways of being lost.

———————

Take Meg now. You might say she was lost the moment she took ship to Ireland in 1649, or even before. How many women have you ever heard of being part of that army? Yet they were there, the women. They always are. But never entering the record, they do not fall out of it. No one missed Meg, because the men on her side died all around her. And hers was the side that won in that conflict. Fat lot of good that did Meg and her brother. They were lost. Meg's brother—his name was Richard—died and was left unburied on that moor in Connacht. But he could still be in heaven now. He was a Puritan. Such men don't need priests and rites when they die. They expect to meet their God, and to be chosen or not chosen. That is the deal they've struck. Meg was born a Puritan but she didn't die one. It wasn't the deal she struck.

Meg was well tired of striking deals by the time she'd been in Ireland two months. This was after the siege of Wexford, when she was no longer a washerwoman. She struck deals in tents and ditches and haystacks. Standing, sitting, lying. Sometimes they were to her advantage, sometimes to the advantage of her clients and adversaries. Many of the men were sick and desperate and terrified like she was. Quite a few were wounded, so if it came to a fight with her, it might end in a draw. Meg was a whore but she wasn't an easy one.

She also saw a lot of people die. Soldiers on both sides,

women, even some children. Her regiment lost their surgeon early on. Whatever doctoring went on was done by the men themselves and their friends and followers. Cooks. Farriers. Laundresses. Meg stanched many wounds following shouted directions. She also delivered a few babies though she was no midwife. Any serious wound always killed a man eventually. Often, quicker was better. Meg found herself, as time went on, doing rounds at night to the wounded like some kind of reverend mother. Odd sort of work for a whore, she thought. Sometimes, these visits of whispered consolation would become fucking: some men were horny right to the very end and died with dirty words on their lips. But more often, Meg found herself just talking to men who were afraid and in pain in the last minutes of their lives. Some talked about God and their expectations of heaven or hell. Some joked. Some reminisced or repeated camp gossip. A surprising number asked her to marry them. They would talk and then they would stop talking; breathe and then stop breathing. In a fragment of a second, time after time, she would go from beholding a person to beholding a body. There was no way to get used to it. It was the same leering absence every time. Something, then nothing. It wore away her faith. Nothing that she witnessed looked like transcendence. It looked like loss. The problem with the afterlife is that it's invisible from life.

So, Meg was confounded to end up on Inis Caillte. But

she was relieved. She did not have to deal with choirs of angels or fire and brimstone. She didn't have to wait around until Judgement Day wondering what had become of her body. She was, as far as she could tell, still herself. Exhausted and despairing, expecting nothing, she received everything, insofar as the contents of consciousness constitute everything.

———

Philip Murphy also got to Inis Caillte. He was staring along the length of a bayonet inches from his chest, held by a twenty-year-old soldier named Jacobus De Jong, when he, as it were, melted away. Philip was surprised, as was the soldier. Both were thankful, though perhaps not equally. De Jong still had to go straight on to the next man in the crowd. It was Brussels in 1830 and he had been called out to quash a rebellion against William I. There was another Irishman in that same crowd named Declan O'Brien, one who in taking monastic orders two years later took the name Anselma. He was only a few ranks away from Philip, almost directly behind him. It may even be that the hesitation Philip's disappearance caused De Jong gave O'Brien enough time to get away. De Jong worried about the lost man later, wondering what had happened to him—but what's one rebel more or less?

Philip, on the other hand, was left worrying about whether he had been involved in a miracle or not. He was not in heaven. The landscape did not answer to the heavenly Jerusalem, and, fresh from his terror, the first thing he had to do was squat down and crap before he ruined his breeches. *Surely, we do not need to shit in heaven.* He certainly was still possessed of his flesh. He wandered on some distance before it occurred to him to stop and pray. This he did but it seemed inconclusive. Whatever had occurred had been so extreme that he felt he was within his rights to expect a bit of a gloss from the divine—even a hint as to how, or why, he had been so suddenly translated. But it did not come.

Philip drifted on until he came to a rocky shore and it occurred to him that he could be on an island. Anxiety rose within him. There are many stories told of islands that Irishmen end up on, and few of them are appropriate for a priest. He might run into a temptress like Circe. Or giants. If he came across a hero who could spurt blood from his ears while one eye grew as round as a plate and the other shrank to the size of a raisin, he, Father Murphy, was not going to know what to say. A nice peaceful little monastery, now, that would fall within his compass. Those were often found on Irish islands too.

He found none of these things. After three days of

wandering, very hungry and getting increasingly frail, he found a farmer. An Irish farmer by the name of Peadar Flaherty. Philip had been encountering the man's sheep for the past two days. He had left them strictly alone. He was the last man on earth—if he was on earth—to steal another man's sheep, though he was a radical. He was probably too feeble to kill one, anyway. Nor was it out of the question that he was undergoing some sort of religious trial, in which case slaughtering a lamb seemed unpropitious. He greeted the farmer and collapsed at his feet. Peadar Flaherty gave him some water and got him into his family's house, where they looked after him for some time. The Flahertys were natives of the island and did their best to explain its peculiarities to him. They were delighted to see a priest, as they hadn't seen one on that side of the island for thirty years, they said. They were happy to hear him read from the Gospels. He had a tiny printed Vulgate with him. Without thinking—his brains were still a bit scrambled—he began to read from John straight off in Latin. *In principio erat verbum.* The whole family followed him apparently with no problem at all, right down to the four-year-old. It was the same with *The Sorrows of Young Werther*, which he happened to have in his other pocket. In German. That gave him pause indeed. He began to wonder if it might not be heaven after all.

The Flahertys helped him to build his cottage. That is, they built it and he carried a few things around, truth be told. They were very hospitable people. He taught the four-year-old, Pádraig, his letters. He presided over one family wedding. Other than that, though, they never asked him to do anything. No blessings. No confessions. No sacraments of any kind. It was odd. "What did you do for marriages before?" he asked Peadar.

"Oh, there's the one priest over on t' other side of the island, if we feel we need him. But more often than not, the two just stand up and plight their troth in the house here, you know. Then we build them a cottage, like we did for you," he replied. And it was true that they were just as interested in *Werther* as in the Bible, if not more so.

"It's a grand book, that one," said Anna, Peadar's mother, the matriarch. "You'd better read it all again."

Philip read the Goethe to them all again. He tried to picture reading a Romantic book about a German suicide to a grandmother of his previous experience—say, one from County Clare. The picture would not form in his mind.

Then he found Nellie.

He smelled rabbit roasting over a hill and walked over, thinking it was likely to be Thomas, Peadar's teenage son, good with a snare. A rabbit of any size is enough for two. Squatting in front of the fire he found a filthy and emaciated girl wearing a fisherman's sweater. When he spoke to her, she understood and tried to reply, but her voice wavered and cracked like a boy undergoing the change. She formed words no better than a toddler might. Yet her understanding was exceedingly quick. She was a mystery.

Nor was her mystery quickly solved when he led her back over the hill to the Flahertys' farm. They took one look at her too-big sweater and called a family council. Not but they fed her first and offered the poor girl a bath, which she refused. Soon the whole twelve of them, including the two hired men, were all crammed into the main room of the cottage, examining the sweater, which was stinking in the heat of the fire. She refused to relinquish it.

"Sure enough it's one of ours," Anna pronounced authoritatively. "From Inis Caillte. Like as not it was Joseph O'Connor's, him who was lost more'n a year ago."

Yes, everyone agreed. Look, the ball—the rope—the cow's hoof. Ours. Ours.

"How did you come by this, girl?" asked Peadar, not unkindly.

"Nellie," said the girl. It was the first and only word she said clearly.

"Nellie," returned Peadar. "You are most welcome here, Nellie. Can you tell us how you came by this sweater? It's from one of our own men. From this island. Inis Caillte."

_____

Nellie could not explain. She was not used to talking; that was clear. She touched her ears, covering them and releasing them, again and again. Finally, Philip understood. "I think she is telling us that once she could not hear. Only now she can. So, maybe she did not speak before, or very little?"

Nellie nodded and lifted her hands in quick assent. After that, it went quicker, by question and answer. It came out that the sweater was from a dead man. He had washed up on the beach of Inis Mór, near her village. An old woman had kept it and Nellie had got it from her. The man had had a decent burial. Everyone murmured with relief. They could tell Clara O'Connor. So, that was all right. Thank heaven.

After a little more urging by the womenfolk, Nellie accepted the bath and was led away to the wash house. The next morning, she yielded up the sweater so it also could be washed. The next time Philip saw her, she was quite transformed. She had accepted gifts of clothing from various Flaherty women. The heavy sweater, which dwarfed her, would take several days to dry, so she was no longer wearing it. Very concerned about it, however, she went to check on it several times a day as it lay spread out in the wash house. "I thought, belike, it had belonged to her man. That maybe she had got together with O'Connor, you know, so it was a relic of his to her. Precious. But I don't think it's that," said Anna to Philip.

"It gives her security, perhaps," said Philip. "Whatever happens to us, the ones who just find themselves here, is so strange and difficult to explain. Or to accept. Anything from home makes us feel safer. I feel like that about my books. I still carry them around," said Philip, apologetically.

"More'n likely it's that sweater brought her here," said Anna, "And you by your books. I've heard people say, the newcomers like yourself, it takes a talisman."

"So, *Werther* brought me here? Or the book of Revelation?"

"That young Werther, he felt despair, seems to me. Enough that he sought a way out of his life. And St John, now, wasn't he an exile on that island there, Patmos? If that book isn't about escape, I don't know what is," said Anna.

Nellie was used to living wild. She was better with a snare even than Thomas. She got on well with Thomas right from the start. He taught her to catch trout in the little river that ran by the house, which she had never done before. She also took right away to little Pádraig. They did a lot of talking together, which helped Nellie a lot. With the women she was cautious, though less so with Anna. As Nellie grew more confident in speech, she told Anna about Aoife. She also told her about her life before. Anna therefore had a good idea about what might be going on with Thomas in addition to fishing for trout, but she kept it to herself. Marriages with newcomers were not uncommon.

Philip was still teaching Pádraig to read. The child's friend Nellie started to come along to lessons, which was fine with him. Literacy is a gift that ought to be offered to all, Philip thought. Nellie learned very fast, and reading words aloud helped her pronunciation. Eventually, Philip asked her about her deafness. "Did it just disappear when you got here?" he asked. "Had you heard nothing before?"

"I lived in a world of silence in Cill Rónáin," said Nellie. "It was only broken when I came here. It was awful. It made me sick at first. I didn't know what it was."

"Did you know what people said, who were talking around you?"

"Some of it. Not all. When they looked right at me, and spoke to me, I could see the words on their mouths."

The idea of seeing words was pleasing to Philip. It was like reading. It was wonderful to think that words could be read even as they were being spoken. "Do you miss it, the silence?" he asked her.

"Sometimes," she replied.

"I can see that," he said, thinking of the bustle of the Flahertys' house.

"Reading is silent, though," she added.

"Yes, it is," he said. They smiled at each other.

Without thinking too much about it, Philip assumed that Nellie would form an attachment to Thomas. The lad was a bit younger than she was, perhaps, but not much. He was confident around her and joked with her. They seemed to speak a mutual language. Anna, in particular, seemed to take it as read that the two would pair off. Philip himself always felt mildly uncomfortable around her. He rather prided himself about advanced ideas that he held, or thought he held, about the emancipation of women. However, having a woman before him who was, in a variety of ways, emancipated, proved to be quite startling. Within a few months, she was able to read *The Sorrows of Young Werther* aloud as well as he could himself. Or, really, better. The torture and despair of Werther, his struggles with his own mood and his sense of unfreedom, came out of Nellie's mouth with complete and unblushing conviction. It made Philip abashed.

The Flaherty house was always very busy, so Philip began to hold lessons for Pádraig and Nellie in his own cottage. This was more convenient as winter came on and more people competed for space indoors, he told himself. They drank nettle and wild mint tea—there was no black tea to be had on the island, and Philip missed it sorely—and talked about things that were of less and less interest to Pádraig. Eventually, the boy begged off and stayed home with his brothers to help with the net-mending and so on. This left the two of them alone. Feeling more and more tense and somehow expectant whenever she was around, Philip finally said to her one day, "I don't know that there's anything more I can teach you, Nellie."

"So, maybe there's something I can teach you," she said. Philip started to blush at that and went on blushing for about three days. At the end of that time, they both emerged from his cottage and went to the Flaherty farm.

Old Anna saw them come over the hill, hand in hand. "Ah," she said. Thomas's heart sank within him. As Philip could not figure out how to preside at his own wedding and nobody wanted to fetch the priest from the other side of the island, he and Nellie stood up before the company and declared that they were married, as the custom was. They had a big dinner with a bit of fiddle music and that was that. Thomas was sad but philosophical. He had always known that there was no way he could compete with Father Murphy if he became a contender.

Philip would lie lazily in bed with Nellie in the morning, amazed at his lack of guilt. He had not previously realized that he had spent his days feeling guilty about almost everything. It occurred to him that this may not have been a requirement of his job as a priest, but he had urgently felt that it was. Perhaps erroneously. He did not feel any less a priest now. It is the part of a priest to guide people towards divinity, to show them the dimension of holiness in things. He continued to be capable of this, as, indeed, did Nellie. She had a rich, meditative mind, capable of deep imaginative associations. Many of the things she said about the relations of people and nature struck him as pure poetry. Perhaps she was a priest too. Of course, this was a blasphemous idea. But he felt less guilt now about blasphemous ideas. There they were. God obviously knew about them. He must have known for millennia. Yet everything carried on. The point of having a mysterious God is that he should be mysterious.

Philip's guilt fell away from him just as Nellie's deafness had fallen away from her. Perhaps guilt is also a kind of deafness.

———————

Mary MacIntosh knit a sweater for her husband as a wedding present. Such was the custom. She began on the day of their betrothal, and the day she finished it they were married. It was a bit of an incentive to knit fast, and so she did. It was just over three months. Philip Murphy married them. Nellie was there, and Meg Haylock, and the Flaherty clan, and all the MacIntosh family. It was a bigger affair than Philip and Nellie's wedding had been.

Mary fell pregnant within two months, and Jim, who had always believed that he hated children, was overjoyed. As summer came on and the weather got milder, he took his currach out fishing more often. As he had a grand total of one and a half cows on his land—a young cow in calf had been the couple's wedding gift from her family—there was not a lot to do on his farm. Mary kept the kitchen garden. So, he took the boat out more, as he had to be doing something. He was not a man for idleness, even as a newlywed. And he loved his little boat. It had been the only thing that ever pleased him, back when he was a curmudgeon. Now that he was recovering from his premature curmudgeonhood, it pleased him even more. He had made it with his own hands. As he floated about on the blue, or the green, or the grey, or the black ocean, he often thought of its little round dot as the pupil of an eye. The roving eye of the sea, looking upwards. The eye, he thought, that had seen Inis Caillte when he could not.

The sea does not care what metaphors we use. It

winked one day and Jim's boat was gone. It was once again immeasurably vast and careless and blind. Jim's wedding sweater snagged on a rock on the north shore of Inis Mór—the shore he had never managed to reach, and rarely even managed to see, for thirteen months. That day, he reached it. His body travelled less than a mile and stretched itself out on the beach as if it were no problem at all. There he lay like a sand dollar, waiting to be claimed. Wavelets ran over him with searching fingers as he lay face up, reading the nubbly surface of his sweater like Braille. Lost. Lost. Lost.

His wife Mary wept and mourned for him when he did not come back to her. She cursed his little boat. She cursed the coast of Inis Mór, which she could barely see through rolling fog.

But if the curses of the lost made islands sink, there would be no islands left.

———

It took Nellie some time to get used to being a married woman. It was odd to have somebody else around all the time. She had been used to going for days without seeing anyone, especially in summer when she had spent less time at old Aoife's. The one item she had insisted on bringing with her to Philip's cottage was the sweater she had brought—or perhaps which had brought her—to the island.

The Flahertys had been reluctant to give it up. It was their opinion that it ought to be given directly to Clara O'Connor, as a memento of her husband. Nellie was not ready for that. She had gotten quite wild on a number of occasions as they tried to persuade her to part with it. Once the sweater had dried from its original washing—which took upwards of a week in that climate—she had always kept it with her. She rarely wore it, except at infrequent times when she was alone, but she kept it draped over her bed, and if she was upset about anything, she would go and huddle there, wrapped in it. Before sleep, she would often lay it flat and trace over its pattern with her hands, sometimes with her eyes closed. She would try to imagine the lives of the sheep from whose wool it had been made. She would think of them wandering, eating salt grass, with their absurdly hairy bodies and thin legs. She would picture the drama of their shearing, how they were rounded up and caught and held, struggling, as their coats were cut off, and then they would bound away, feeling strangely light and small. Then their stinky fleeces would be washed and dried and carded and spun into yarn, and then knitted. Nellie pictured human hands doing this. She avoided thinking about Clara O'Connor, whose hands they must have been.

This sweater had come to her. It had saved her. What

did it have to do with Clara O'Connor? Now? Why would she even want it? After all, it had not saved her husband. No, it had saved her, Nellie. Hers was the greater claim. Life is more important than death.

When she moved to Philip's house with him, she kept the sweater folded neatly on a shelf in their bedroom. She would often touch it, patting it lightly, as she went in or out of the room. Philip remarked on this. "It's a relic of yours," he would say. "A touchstone. I've seen reliquaries like that, you know, with shiny patches on them from all the hands touching them over the years." He used to joke that it would end up threadbare. Nellie did not like to think of it threadbare.

However, as the months went on with Philip, her husband, and her new life in their cottage, her mind began to dwell on Clara O'Connor. She tried to avoid thinking about her, but her thoughts became more and more insistent. Clara had been married too. She had been married for a far longer time than Nellie, for years and years, and she had two children. They were teenage boys now, according to Anna Flaherty. *So!* said a triumphant voice in Nellie's head, *see! She has two sons! What would she need an old sweater for?* Nellie tried to bolster up this voice, but it was slowly and steadily drowned out by a rising conviction that she had to go and see Clara O'Connor, and talk to her … and, finally, give her back the sweater that her husband had worn to sea. Nellie shed many tears over this conviction. She tried to make it go away but she couldn't.

At length, she talked to Philip about it. He agreed, gently, that they should go and talk to Clara, and at least show her the sweater. So, one autumn day, they set out. Clara lived quite far away. It was a good three hours' walk. Nellie carried the sweater in her arms, clutched tight against her chest. Philip looked at her pityingly but was quiet. They walked all that way with very little conversation.

When they got to the O'Connors' door, Nellie said she would like to go in alone. Philip nodded. He went and sat on the garden wall, and waved to her to go on. Nellie released one hand from the sweater and knocked on the door.

A tall, fair woman with a tired, lined face opened the door. "Clara O'Connor? Clara?" said Nellie. The woman gave the faintest, briefest nod at that name. Nellie, biting her lips hard, thrust the folded sweater suddenly into the woman's hands. There were damp patches on it from her sweaty hands. The woman looked down, surprised.

"I am Nellie," said Nellie to Clara O'Connor. Clara looked at her quickly, shrewdly. She knew that name. She gathered the wool against her chest and turned to go in. But she did not close the door.

"Come in," she said. Nellie hesitated. She heard the woman's skirts swishing across the room. She breathed deeply and went in the door. Clara had the sweater spread out on the kitchen table. She was looking down at it silently, with both palms flat on it. Her face was as pale as paper in a book. She said nothing but Nellie saw her hands trembling on the wool.

"I know it is yours," said Nellie. "I am sorry I kept it. I couldn't help it."

"'Tis no matter," replied the woman, though Nellie could see that, of course, it was a great matter. People say such things. Clara was silent another moment. "Thank you for bringing it," she said. Suddenly, her knees seemed to give, and she sat down on a kitchen chair with a thump and gathered the sweater up before her on the table, pressing her face into it, clutching it with her hands. All the time, she remained so silent that Nellie thought she had been struck deaf again. But there had been the little thump as she hit the chair, and the woman's shallow breathing. She moved tentatively forward and touched Clara O'Connor's shoulder. Under her hand, the woman's flesh was trembling and trembling, almost vibrating.

"I should go now," said Nellie.

"No," said Clara.

"Where are your children?" said Nellie. "Do you want me to fetch them?"

"Working," replied Clara. She sat up, holding the sweater to her. "I'll show it to them later. They'll be amazed, amazed to have something of his. Joseph's. Something that he touched, and wore. We've had nothing."

"But didn't he sit on that chair, and build these walls, and everything?" asked Nellie.

"He did. He did," said Clara, looking around, bewildered. "But this is the thing. I've been waiting for it ever since I heard what happened."

Nellie's eyes filled with tears but her voice was steady. She felt that if she gave way, Clara would too, and that the woman would be embarrassed. "Well, here it is," she said. "Now you have it. It saved my life, and now it's come back to you."

"I'll tell you about him, shall I?" said Clara. "Seeing as he wore it before you did?"

"I want to know," said Nellie, simply.

So, Clara O'Connor talked for two hours about her husband. Nellie thought briefly about Philip waiting outside on the wall. He was a patient man. She decided to let him be patient. Clara told her that she and Joseph had known each other since childhood. They were second cousins. Cousin marriages were common on such a small island. He had been tall and fair, like her. Easygoing. Kind. An excellent father. An excellent farmer. Good with beasts and children. He rarely fished. It had not even been his boat that he had been lost in. He had borrowed it from a neighbour. Clara had been worrying about paying the neighbour back ever since for the boat, though he had told her it was unnecessary. Joseph had only gone out because there had been an unusually rich herring run. He just couldn't let the opportunity go, he had said, what with those two boys growing so fast. "You know, I was even angry with the boys about it," said Clara, her voice shaking. "I was cold to them, I was so angry. I'm ashamed of it now."

Nellie murmured consolingly. Clara went on. She went on for a long time. She tried to keep a stern countenance, but gradually tears spilled down her face. Nellie understood that Clara had loved her husband deeply and that she missed him constantly and silently. They had been married for such a long time that they had been like one person, and now half that person was missing. Clara felt that she was hobbling around on one leg. And the boys were joyless and lonely. Anthony, the younger one, was still hardly sleeping; he came into his mother's bed almost every night in the wee hours with his cheeks wet. Michael, the fifteen-year-old, was laconic. He got into nasty fights with his old friends. Their mother was terribly worried about both of them. Nellie was not sure that a sweater was going to rectify these things. Still, seeing Clara's hands stroking and stroking it as she spoke, Nellie felt that it was offering her something. She had spent hours doing exactly the same thing herself.

Nellie let Clara talk herself out. Then she rose and patted the exhausted woman's shoulder. Clara stayed seated. She looked too weak to get up. "Thank you," she said. "Thank you, Nellie." Nellie nodded and motioned for her to stay where she was.

"I should go now," said Nellie. "Philip is waiting. I am sorry that I waited so long to return this precious thing to you. I couldn't let it go. But I have now. Good luck to you, Clara O'Connor." She left Clara sitting there, worn out.

Philip was waiting, patiently, on the garden wall. He joined her quietly and they began to walk home. "You gave it to her, Nellie," he said. "That was brave. I have never given up my books, have I?"

Nellie smiled at him wanly. "Well," she said, "other people use your books, don't they? Not just you."

"Still," said Philip, "it was brave."

They walked home. Nellie went to bed. She was too tired to eat, too tired to talk. Philip did not insist on either. When she walked into the bedroom, she saw that in the empty place on the shelf where the sweater had been, there was a mug of wild flowers. She gazed at it for a while and then fell asleep.

When she woke up, very early the next morning, her head was full of words. She was not sure what to make of them. They were mostly Clara O'Connor's words about her husband, strangely changed. It was like a song, running in her mind, but without music. She let it run there for a while and then told Philip about it.

"Try writing it down," he said.

"You and your books! Writing!" said Nellie. "What would I write it on?"

"The end-papers of *Werther*?" suggested Philip. "Or maybe I could make you a wax tablet, such as schoolboys use?"

"With what wax, Philip?" said Nellie.

"Yes, well," said Philip, defeated, "perhaps you could just say the words for me?"

Nellie said the words. Philip sat very still. "Again," he said. Philip was a literate man. He knew Irish, Latin, German, Flemish and some French and English. He had grown up with Irish poems and songs; he had learned Latin scripture and hymns. He was compassionate and he had a good ear. "Again," he said.

Nellie spoke the words again. "Holy Ghost, Nellie," he said. "Do you know what you've done? You've gone and composed a lament for Joseph O'Connor, and it's the best I've ever heard. Jesus, Mary, and ... Joseph ... Nellie, it's like the *Lament for Art O'Leary*. But without the horses or the fine clothes or the beaver hats. And no killer but the sea and the small house and the hunger of his sons. And even the women arguing, Nellie—is that you and Clara? Claiming the sweater while his body spins in the sea? Jesus, Nellie!"

Nellie did not entirely know what he was talking about. But soon enough she learned. Philip told her many things. He wrote poems that he recalled down for her. He spoke them. Their greatest gift in all of this was discovering a small stretch of beach covered with sand. Fine sand. So you could write on it with a stick or a rock. A clean slate, at least until the tide came in. Nellie would think of things, organize them in her head, and Philip would write them. Eventually, she herself would write them. Sometimes. Often, she preferred just to say them. Philip never preferred this. He was a scholar.

He started killing sheep. Or even calves. Or trading for their skins. Anything, everything. Teaching all kinds of lessons, just to get hold of material on which to write down Nellie's poems.

Nellie was surprised. She did not know how to put a value on such things. Was it worth killing calves? But she found, once she had got it straight in her head—the pattern she had made out of Clara's words—that she no longer missed the sweater. That told her. What she herself had made had gone into the place of it, filled it up. Nothing else had been able to. Not the love of Philip. Not her house, or her comfortable life. It had been seeing the relief of Clara, and letting go of the sweater herself, and all the things it had meant, and substituting for them her own words, in a tight pattern. One that stuck in her mind and held things together. So, she accepted that her first poem had been *The Lament for Joseph O'Connor*. She took a copy of it that Philip had made to Clara, who was rendered speechless. She went on from there.

———————

It wasn't the curse of the wretched widow Mary Conneely that made any difference to Inis Mór. It wasn't the curse of Clara O'Connor, either, whose husband had washed ashore there the previous year.

It was the poison.

That's the thing about islands. We think we're safe on them. Separate. The sea is a *cordon sanitaire*. Alas, anything that washes up can bring contagion, including the bodies of men. In this case, it wasn't typhoid or plague, as at St Kilda's or Mingulay. It was despair. Despair is widely spoken of as poisonous, but with as little meaning as words have when we use them to describe pain. Pain is something of which we can only observe the effects. Despair is similar. One of the effects of despair was to bring people—newcomers—to Inis Caillte. Suddenly. Somehow. It opened a door for them. But some doors, once opened, are hard to close.

What did become of Nellie's despair as she lay silently dying? Of Jim's, as he was about to drown? Of Meg's, or Philip's? We might say they carried it with them. They brought it with them in their despairing flesh, and when they touched the island of Inis Caillte—when they, as it were, grounded—their despair flashed straight out of them into the earth. So they were rid of it. The island filtered it out of them. But it wasn't gone. It was in the soil, permeating everything. The natives were used to it. Newcomers had been bringing their burdens of despair to the island for generations. If the Flahertys and the MacIntoshes and everybody else had not been able to process it, they would have long since died off. But it was quite another thing when a bodily person belonging to the island ended up somewhere else.

From the buried bodies of Jim Conneely and Joseph O'Connor despair began to spread. They were men of Inis Caillte, one by birth and one by adoption. Despair was—what?—active in them, operative? It was part of them, a factor of their lostness. As they decomposed, it leached straight into the ground, that thin layer of precious soil that, perhaps uniquely in the Arans, is already a composite of despair. After all, people had lugged the dirt of Inis Mór, spadeful by spadeful, to every inch of field and garden.

At the same time, the earth of the Aran islands was made out of things from the margins of the sea, even directly from the sea itself. Sand. Seaweed. Fish. We might call that unnatural. It was at once a great triumph and a great risk. The first victim of the resulting poison was Mary Mullen.

The beautiful, light-stepping Mary Mullen was known to visit the grave of the unknown fisherman—Joseph O'Connor—from time to time when she was feeling sentimental. She also laid a posy or two on Jim Conneely's grave. Like everyone else, she had thought Jim handsome and cold. Bitter. There wasn't much to miss about him, but he was dead, and the dead do deserve some looking after.

Mary wasn't exactly commended for this, though a few people when either prayerful or drunk said that it spoke to her sense of religion. This was not the view taken by Jim Conneely the younger, however. "It's like she's practicin' to be a widow," he said. He was jealous, pure and simple.

Mary also kept up her interest in the mystery of the sweater pattern that had appeared twice among them in such sad circumstances. In this she was like Arthur O'Donnell, and it's a shame that neither of them knew about the other. It might have led to some mitigation. Mary even talked to Mairín about it, and saw the copy that Arthur had made. Mairín, however, neglected to mention this to Arthur, who was out fishing that day. The baby choked and drove it clean out of her head. Mary didn't have a memory like Mairín's, but she did recall a few big things. A round ball. Something that looked like the letter M. And a lot of cable or cord, which she knew from other women was supposed to be fishermen's rope. She made up many a grand tale about them. She could almost bring herself to tears. The ball was a pomander of sweet spices such as noblewomen carry in French stories. God knows it would be a wonderful thing on these islands with their smell of cow shit and herring. The letter M would sometimes stand for Mary, though she fought against that temptation. If it seemed too selfish, she could always remind herself how many Marys there are on the islands. A heroic fisherman with a rope could do practically anything, not least rescue either Mary or the lady with the pomander from drowning. Or fish, of course. This was overwhelmingly likely to be the most important meaning, as she well knew, given that the purpose of the patterns was to attest to the way of life of the men who wore them. As a clue, though, it left much to be desired. Fishing was not likely to narrow things down.

Mary steadily turned down a variety of offers of marriage, some realistic and others not. Jim Conneely the younger was one of the latter. He was only fifteen and should have known better. He took a lot of ribbing for it. He apologized to his mates for losing his head. He even apologized to Mary. She was very gracious about it.

Mary was very gracious in everything. Graciously, she began to withdraw. Graciously, she let people down. She missed appointments. She missed church. She missed the baptism of her sister's child. She was sweet. She was apologetic. She was never, ever rude. She absolutely had not meant to do it. Had not meant to hurt anyone. She wouldn't. She would never.

She became the girl who would never. For the younger Jim Conneely, it was terrible to watch. She was four years older than he was. He saw her go from a lovely girl of nineteen to a creature that seemed sometimes a crone, sometimes an infant. She slipped out of time. It was not so very drastic, not to other people's eyes, but he would catch an old woman, exhausted, careworn, peering out of her eyes, or see the smug, placid gaze of a child much younger than either of them fleetingly occupy her face. She talked about the usual things but without conviction. She lost weight but could not be said to be wasting away like a doomed sweetheart in a ballad. It wasn't like that. It was subtle and deep and horrible. Something had infected her. That was how Jim thought of it. She was like a dog whose master has died. Those dogs are weird. They go on living but something goes out of them.

It's hard to say how much other people noticed. They saw her make more and more of her visits to the graveyard. Always to the unknown man now. She had abandoned the deceased Jim Conneely. He had kin. The younger Jim Conneely almost wished it was his dead uncle she was visiting. He would have been able to dig him up and fight a duel with him, or something. With this unknown fellow, there was nothing to get hold of.

He watched Mary making her visits from time to time. She did not appear to care, though he thought she did notice. It was not that she fell swooning and weeping on the man's grave. She just stood there quietly, wrapped in a billowing private silence. Sometimes, Jim fancied he saw it blowing and swirling around her like rags or tatters. Perhaps she would wipe away a tear. Occasionally, he saw her lips move. But he could not rid himself of the notion that she was being filled up with something, taking it in, perhaps through the soles of her feet on the earth, or through the pores of her skin. Infection. Decay. Death. A few times, driven to desperation, he went over to her, tried to get her to come away. They would talk of this and that, politely, but she would not go with him. Graciously, she would refuse. She would only be there for a few more minutes. The poor man. The poor man.

Jim saw her do these things. He knew that she was suffering, perhaps suffering greatly. He was not able to

understand why. Nor could Mary, in truth. Despair is be-
fuddling. Her feelings were strangely elongated and slow.
The circumstances of her life had not changed, yet she,
in herself, was completely different. Everyone and everything seemed sad to her. People might look superficially
happy but she saw through to their dark cores. What was
there, after all, to be happy about? All things were imper-
manent. Death was everywhere. People hardly ever got
what they wanted. What she wanted was to meet and
know this man whose grave she haunted, and he was un-
meetable and unknowable. There was no way whatsoever
around this problem. Not in life. Not in death. She still
would not meet him if she were dead, would she? It is
commonly said that despair drives people towards death.
In fact, it renders death worthless. The despairing may
stumble upon death, perhaps, but it is an event without
meaning. Meaninglessness welled up out of the ground
and spread as a vapour in the damp air, and Mary drank
it in. It took up residence in every cell of her body. It dis-
placed her and destroyed her. Her will failed. All contest,
all risk, all chance, all change became nothing. There was
a dull uniformity within and without her. A nullity without distinction.

As this went on, she remained curiously cheerful and
sweet-tempered, outwardly. She did not blame or rant or
curse. She withdrew from people, but when she chanced

to meet them, she seemed the kind and considerate girl she had been. It was as if her body remembered the forms and words and attitudes of politeness, compassion, interest. Mary was, in fact, a good and strong person. Good at being a person. Well brought up. Virtuous habit kept her together, right to the end. Even after a year, when she was merely a void in the shape of a girl, when Mary spoke to people in the street, she spoke decently. She spoke pleasantly when she could no longer even hear herself speak, when there was no difference between speaking and not speaking. When all difference had disappeared.

There was a reason for this, and that reason was the nature of Joseph O'Connor. He had been a sweet-tempered man. His body rotted into the ground, and the despair that grew out of him was tinged with sweetness. Every kind of person can produce despair, not just the proud or the cold or the black-hearted. Despair is an element in humans. Perhaps it is acid, perhaps alkaline. There is something about living on Inis Caillte that renders it volatile. In these strange days that came over Inis Mór—when a force usually passive became active, and despair burst its human bonds to spread into the earth itself—people learned that individuals decay into differing varieties of despair. All despair is poison and its essence is undifferentiation, so how different could they be? Not very. Just a little. Just enough that the lingering touch of sweetness belonging to Joseph O'Connor, native of Inis Caillte, combined with the last faltering sweetness of Mary Mullen to allow her to be gracious to her last breath, though eaten up entirely from the inside.

Jim Conneely the younger, just turned sixteen, saw Mary Mullen die. She had gone to lay flowers on the unknown fisherman's grave, as on any other day. She stood there quietly. As the lad looked at her, her outline blurred and shifted. It suddenly sagged and collapsed in on itself. Mary was gone. Jim ran forward with a cry to find a scattering of black earth, smelling of seaweed and fish and dung. It was as if the grave had turned itself inside out. But when Jim looked at the plot with its modest stone, it was undisturbed. The dirt was Mary. She had not been able to retain her own shape any longer. The despairing earth had rendered her into itself. It knew no difference.

Jim did not touch the spilled earth. He did not touch the grave. He gave a great keening scream and ran sobbing home. No one wanted to believe his story, but eventually they had to.

Some people are far more dangerous dead than alive, and Jim Conneely was one of them. He had lived his whole life as a malcontent and was only just beginning to turn into something else when he met his end. His friends and family were not wrong when they identified him as cold and bitter. Bitter he had been. Bitterness prevailed in him, and it rotted out of him as he returned to the earth.

Young Jim, his nephew, had spent a lot of time spying on Mary in the churchyard. He took her death very hard. He had a hard time persuading those in the village, particularly Father Anselma, to grant Mary a proper funeral. Nellie had had no funeral in Cill Rónáin either. When women are lost, it is less likely that monuments will be erected to their memories. Jim had finally yelled at the priest, "Earth to earth, Father! Earth to earth, like you say in the service! So you might as well put your blessing on it!" Father Anselma had reluctantly agreed. He did not accept Jim's story. It was not the line of country in which he was prepared to believe. He thought Mary had run off, but as she turned up nowhere on a small island, he considered it at least very possible that she was dead. There was pressure from the family. So, he conceded and held a service. He reflected as he did so that the whole question of funerals in Cill Rónáin was a vexed one.

Jim had shown Mary's parents, and others, the scattered black earth. No one was willing to touch it. They left it be, and eventually green grass grew over it. It became indistinguishable from the rest of the churchyard soil, which consisted, after all, mostly of decomposed humans. Jim thought of this more and more acutely as he went about his business in the village and on the farm. The only time these thoughts would leave him was when he was out in a boat. The earth was deadly. It was made up of dead things. Dead plants. Dead fish. Dead people. Potatoes lay nestled in the ground, feeding on death. Grass stems grew out of it. It was horrific.

Jim decided that he was the enemy of all dirt. He was at war with the ground. He was glad to see cattle trample it. He rejoiced to see it cut up by ploughs and wounded by spades. He walked on it only by sufferance. He took to stealing out at night and sleeping in the family boat. Mary was in the ground, was part of the ground. He hated her, too. She had abandoned him for a dead man.

Gradually, people noticed that the young Jim Conneely was becoming a lot like his uncle. Taciturn. Standoffish. Harsh. He had always been an easygoing boy. His mother and father and three brothers began to feel that they were living with a different person. "Whatever's wrong, Jim?" his mother kept asking.

"It's nothing. There's nothing!" he would say. Nobody was satisfied with this but it's all they got.

Jim, like his uncle before him, picked fights. He became expert at the kind of brief, scathing insult that keeps people up at night. He set his brothers up for feuds that would last for years. People began to avoid him. His mates slipped away and he found himself increasingly isolated. This was fine with him. People were just walking dirt, anyway.

As Jim became more and more outwardly bitter, he became more inwardly calm. At last he understood his uncle's cold repose that had so repelled him as a boy. The elder Jim had seen that the world was empty. It seemed full but it was empty. There was an enormous amount of stuff and it was organized in different ways but it added up to nothing. People occupied themselves with the rituals of eating and praying and courtship until they were swallowed by the ground. In the world, there was nothing to be concerned with. When he left it, there would be nothing to miss.

Anyone who has ever lived in a village will know how much harm one bloody-minded person can do, even in a short life. Jim became that person. People stopped calling him "the young Jim Conneely" to distinguish him from his uncle. The two had collapsed together. In fact, it is likely that the memory of the elder Jim was poisoned by the younger one. Mary Conneely, Jim's widow on Inis Caillte, would have been horrified to know what was going on. Neither of these Jim Conneelys had been the man she knew. That Jim's legacy on his home island would come to this would have broken her heart. You see how it is. It is always possible to lose the lost again.

Finally, it ended for Jim as it had done for Mary. He

was walking through the main street of the village with a creel of potatoes on his back. To him, the potatoes were a deadly burden. He made a mocking comment to Thomas Derrane as he passed by. And then, with Thomas still looking right at him and wondering what to say, Jim exploded. There was a muffled whump and there was nothing left of Jim but a pile of damp black earth.

You can see how this might go on, and it did go on. Jim's mother had loved him, and feared for him, right to the end. She swept up the earth from the village street and carried it to the graveyard, where she sprinkled it on the grave of Mary Mullen. Then she began to despair.

———————

A lot of nonsense is talked about the walking dead. As early as 1819, people began to use the Afric word *zombi* in English, then in Irish. To have a *zombi,* you must have a necromancer. There has never been a necromancer on the Aran islands, unless you want to count the priests, who do imagine themselves to be controlling the souls of the dead. Now, a necromancer, like any evil man, can create despair in others. He can torment them and make their lives not worth living. He can kill them. But if he were to bring their bodies back and have them walk around to do his bidding, what does that have to do with despair?

Despair is a condition of the living.

We are little used to the idea of despair accomplishing anything. This seems antithetical to its nature. Yet for some reason, when Meg Haylock despaired on the battle-field of Cromwell's army, when Jim despaired in his boat or Philip Murphy at the point of a bayonet, each wound up on Inis Caillte. This is unfair. Untold millions have despaired at such moments and died. Was there something different in the quality of their despair? Maybe some infinitesimal thing, some shade akin to the bitterness or sweetness that precipitated out of the buried bodies on Inis Mór. Maybe there was a purity to it. They achieved selflessness and were given back their selves. But if we are in these deep waters and we say this, what do we say about the terror that followed? This creeping malaise that got into the ground and infected the innocent? Despair is in us. It is not supposed to be outside us.

Tit for tat. If despair is endowed with energy, energy it will have. If we want to save Meg and Jim and Philip, and keep Inis Caillte hidden as a refuge for the lost, we must pay something. Something, as it were, to recompense the souls of the despairing whom we do not intend to save. Those who disappear into invisible inertia. Momentum gathers on their behalf, building and building and building. The earth itself, the shocking amount of it, absorbs their agency as it has absorbed them. For there is no doubt that the earth we walk on, the cultivated earth, contains a dangerously high percentage of human misery. So, just for this short time, we will witness its despair in action, concentrated into the scant soil of these two small islands.

We are the necromancers here. We have made a golem of the whole earth.

———————

Things and people went on peacefully on Inis Caillte. Nellie stayed out of boats and never returned to Inis Mór. Over time—she lived a long life—she became the most famous poet in the island's history. The language that she composed in was Irish, for the most part, but she also composed in German, which she had learned from *Werther*. However, no one on the island had any trouble understanding the German poems. Or, at least, they understood them as well as they did the Irish ones. The gift of the Lost Isle gave them that much.

Nellie's poems were hard to understand. That was the fact of it. She did not mind. Truth be told, she cultivated their difficulty. Much as she loved her new home, and her new life as a hearing person and her loving husband Philip and all the rest of it, there were times when she felt hard done by. That all this cheap and cheerful communication by mouth was just too much. She fought against it. She fought the translating nature of the island itself by composing exceedingly complicated poetry. Irish is a good language for this. It always annoyed her that Meg, for instance, must hear her poems in English, for as far as she was able to understand it from Meg and Philip, English was a simpleminded language. Not that Meg was big on poetry to begin with.

Many poets say that they write poems. That's not what Nellie said. She composed them, completely, silently, in her head. She finished them there. Then she wrote them down, or some of them. Some she only recited, and others remembered them and wrote them down. Some she spoke aloud and they never got written down and so were lost. And a few she kept always in her own head, quiet. So those ones, too, were lost, but not to her.

She found that, for better or worse, she composed better when she could not hear external sounds. She used little pads of wool to block her ears sometimes, though these made her ears itch. She used compressed thistledown or dandelion seed when they were in season. It always amused her to think of the seeds in her ears. She used to imagine them growing into her brain, and flowers sprouting out her opposite ear. Just as, she said to Philip, the words eventually sprouted out of her mouth. Perhaps they were her co-authors. The sheep.

The seeds. This was the kind of observation that kept Philip in awe of her.

Nellie and Philip had no children. Nellie suspected that her illness had burned that capacity out of her. Philip would have loved children, but he loved Nellie and that was enough for him. Almost enough, anyway. Over the years, he persuaded her to stop using the joking honorific "Father" that she came out with sometimes, as it made him sad. He was the one who kept the records of her poems. He penned a whole shelf of books and looked upon them paternally. Nellie, he thought, was careless of her gift. Or perhaps the dual nature of her gift—on the one side, the urge to express, and on the other, to occlude—too often tipped the latter way. She was content to let poems be lost. It was his duty to gather up as many of them as possible for posterity, so that future readers could wrestle with whatever was lost and found in them, whatever language they turned up in.

Philip, too, stayed on Inis Caillte and spread no poison abroad. Even if after a while he no longer wanted to be called Father, he still considered himself a priest. A servant of the deity. He read the Bible with any interested parties. He presided over the odd wedding or funeral with great reverence and gusto. Most of the other sacraments seemed to have gone by the wayside. He didn't really miss them, though he worried from time to time about baptisms. They were considered so vitally necessary everywhere else. But it's not like there were vast numbers of children born on the island, and those he was closest to he would never have dreamt of baptizing. These were the children of Jim Conneely—whose shade would have risen up out of the ground to choke Philip at the very idea if it were not for the fact that it was unfortunately in the ground of Inis Mór choking his old compatriots at the time—and Mary, and Meg's children.

Mary bore twins seven months after Jim's disappearance. As it happens, Meg helped her out with the birth. She never claimed to be a midwife, but she had some experience with the whole process. Babies sprout up around armies. Her presence was very reassuring to Mary, and Mary called the girl child Meg—Margaret—after her. She felt certain that Jim would have liked this. The boy was called Conor, after her uncle. It was a family name. Meg had two children, both boys. Thomas Flaherty, with whom she kept company for a time, was the father of one of them, and of the other, she would never say. The two of them, Andrew and Christopher, lived with her on her farm and were a great help to her. Their farm prospered, and when a new variety of wheat sprang up upon it, one that they cultivated and stored and re-seeded as it was wonderfully dense and fruitful, they became quite wealthy. Meg's son Christopher became the next miller of Inis Caillte. He was very good with ratchets and cogs and wheels. By careful examination of Philip's pocket watch—the only other thing Philip had had with him, except his clothes and his books—Christopher was able to bring their mill into the nineteenth century. Meg was very proud of him for this, for after all, she said, he probably ought to be accounted a seventeenth-century person.

"No, no!" said Philip, and others shouted her down too. Mary. Conor MacIntosh—Old Conor, as he'd come to be called after the birth of Mary's boy. And various others. No, they all said, some joking, some serious, he's a man of Inis Caillte. We have no such times here.

"Bah," said Meg.

———————

Arthur O'Donnell heard about the deaths of Mary and young Jim, and his heart went cold within him. He was certain that it all had something to do with those lost-and-found men and their too-familiar but unknown sweater panels. Too near, yet too far. But who would believe him? Nobody. Nobody, the friend of fools and beggars.

"We should dig them up. Those strangers. Or that stranger and Jim. Throw whatever's left in the ocean," he insisted. But this was ridiculous and nobody listened to him. Father Anselma pointed out that such a thing would be sacrilege. "Better sacrilege than whatever's going on here," Arthur muttered. But nothing of the kind was done. What was the point of blaming dead men? It was bound to be some kind of sickness. Or maybe, some whispered anxiously, the judgement of God.

The priest was called on to bless this and that. He sprinkled holy water on various headstones and on various children and even on various boats. No one asked him to bless livestock, thank God, as it was obvious that only people were afflicted. By now, many people in the town were acting out of character. Soon enough, there were three more deaths. Every person is missed in a community that small. On a small, harsh island, every person works and every hour of labour is necessary. Cill Rónáin was in serious danger. Father Anselma drew the line at exorcisms, however. He had never performed one and considered them showy. Plus, he knew that if he did even one, the demand would never end. Under strain, people see devils everywhere. And he didn't feel too solid about it doctrinally. It was convention to blame the world, the flesh and the devil. What was he to do if these categories were collapsing? If, for example, the world, the very dirt, was becoming devilish? Or the flesh worldish, turning into earth far too rapidly? He wrote a long, worried letter to the Archbishop of Dublin and one to the Carmelite

Order. He never heard back from either and was left with his conundrums.

Arthur, meanwhile, got out the parchment with Mairín's drawing on it. He pinned it to the wall of the cottage. He felt it was a talisman, like the mark over the door for the Hebrew Passover. He stared at it constantly, running over it in his mind. He was convinced that some sort of solution lay in it. What was the obvious remedy for a rebellion of the soil? For a plague of killing sadness? Should he bury the vellum in the ground? In the grave-yard, perhaps, to combat those two men festering there? He was surprised at himself for this morbid turn of mind.

"Look, Mairín," he said, "d'ye think you could knit this pattern back into a sweater?"

"No," she replied, "I'm no great knitter. But Ma could."

So, after some hemming and hawing, he asked his aunt, could she knit a sweater for him, with the pattern on it? She wasn't keen. "'S bad luck, seems to me," she said. But he persuaded her. It was going to be a long job, though. Two months at least. "See if you can knit it any faster yourself, then!" she said to him when he looked doubtful. He begged her to hurry.

Jim's mother fell sick. She withdrew from her family and made cruel remarks. She criticized her other sons. She mocked her husband for his continual praying over the memory of Jim. "He wouldn't have thanked you for it," she said. "You know he was a right heathen." Her husband wept. He feared what was coming.

Six weeks after Jim's death, Aislinn Derrane—Jim's mother's cousin and best friend from girlhood—walked into her sickroom with a cup of broth to find a wet mess of earth in her bed. There was a powerful smell of seaweed and salt in the room. Aislinn screamed in horror and ran for the rest of the family. They were barely even surprised.

Arthur heard of this immediately, as everyone did. He nagged his aunt. She said she'd finished the blasted front panels, those with the pictures on, and if he wanted the rest done faster, he'd have to ask Mairín, as God knows young women had nothing to do.

So, he begged Mairín to get on with the back and sleeves. Mairín was none too pleased about this but she did it. When Mairín finished the rather lumpy sweater, he wore it. He practically snatched it off her needles and paraded it through town. He told everyone he met all about it. How he had killed the calf. How he had preserved Mairín's picture of the pattern. How the women had made it back into a sweater for him. People thought he was mad, touched by the trouble. These quiet men, you know, they're often weak-minded.

He wore it into the village pub and explained that it had the power to ward off evil. They told him he was drunk.

He wore it to church. Father Anselma looked at it with instant suspicion. He felt that Aoife was taunting him from beyond the grave. What nonsense was the man about to stir up in the midst of a crisis? He spoke severely against foolish superstitions and idols from the pulpit. He spoke of the duty of remorse and prayer. The cross was the only symbol in which to trust at such times of trial.

Aislinn Derrane died. She had been a dour sort of woman, really. Suddenly, in the last two weeks of her life, she was possessed of the kind of mordant gallows humour that had always characterized Jim's mother, her much funnier cousin and best friend. She crumbled into muddy earth while pinning up the washing, and her last words were a bleak quip about it.

Arthur wore the sweater almost all the time, and draped it over his bed at night. It seemed the safest thing. It wasn't just for himself, he told Mairín—he wanted to set an example.

The two youngest Derrane children died, those closest to their mother. They were five and nine. Timothy and Feargal. They had been perfectly healthy boys, not so much as a sniffle, and very high-spirited. In their last days, they were solemn as doorposts, and then they were gone, horribly, *whump,* into small twin piles of dirt.

Arthur wore the sweater to their funeral. Father Anselma's eyes blazed at him. But a few women, all mothers, approached him after the service and asked to see the pattern.

The whole town turned out for that funeral. Thereafter, the poison began to spread like a storm tide, creeping over the land ever faster. There were brawls and beatings and possibly even a murder. Lovers and friends and family stopped talking to one another. Over the next two months, nine people from Cill Rónáin and the surrounding parish disappeared into stinking piles of wet dirt. Despair touched nearly everyone.

Just not the O'Connors. They were a large clan who lived on a large farm with two farmhouses. There were eighteen of them all told, related in various ways. They were all untouched. People noticed. They began to show up in ones and twos, and then in droves, to see Arthur's sweater with Mairín's—Aoife's—pattern on it, and to ask him about it. Arthur was its tireless advocate. He was in the grip of a powerful conviction that he could not explain. Moreover, the sweater's warding magic seemed to be working. His household was safe. They had been passed over. He showed the pattern to everyone who wanted to see it. Many desperate women took the pattern home either in their heads or sketched out in charcoal on anything they could find. Bed linen. Potato sacks. Pet-

ticoats. The whole parish was a fury of knitting needles.
Women stayed home from church, passing skeins
around, spinning any scraps of wool left unspun, unpick-
ing old—and even new—garments. Father Anselma was
not impressed. His flock was straying. He searched for
other metaphors, ones that did not involve sheep. But
fewer and fewer people came to hear his sermons
regardless.

Sheep were shorn out of season. Sheep were stolen.
Soon, it seemed there was not a scrap of yarn to be had
on the entire island. A few men even learned to knit. Still,
as every household in Cill Rónáin and its environs got its
sweater—at least one, and some got many—gradually, it
seemed that the tide slowed. The black despair ceased to
strike. Throughout the whole next year, people kept turning up at the O'Connors with gifts of butter and cheese.
And wool. Mairín and her mother could have opened a
shop with the amount of wool, raw and spun, that they
were given after the next spring shearing. Though they
would never have dreamed of doing such an ill-omened
thing as selling a gift. Arthur became a celebrity. In under
a year, he was headman of the village. He had always
been a quiet sort of man until his enthusiasm for the
sweater, and after that wore off, he remained one. The village council was none the worse for that.

Many men in Cill Rónáin were more considerate of

their wives and daughters, who had knit them out of deadly danger. The old adage was trotted out much more than usual, how a good woman is a shield to her family. Mairín was much praised, and made an excellent marriage. People also, in retrospect, praised old Aoife for having the sense to preserve the sweater from the first lost fisherman so that Mairín could see it. Even some of the crusty old men praised her. People began to talk of re-thatching her cottage so that it might be lived in again. It must be said that Father Anselma lost a bit of ground, but most people eventually forgave him.

In light of the uncanny events that had overtaken them, people wondered all the more what had happened to Nellie, who had disappeared with the original sweater that Aoife had kept. Surely, she could not have turned to black earth herself—not with the sweater on? Had it carried her off somewhere? Where had she gone? Many agreed that it was likely she had gone to the island that the sweater had come from, the home of the mysterious pattern. Some hoped that she might return, armed with knowledge, and explain to them how it was that it had saved them—or even, how it was they had been under threat in the first place.

But Nellie did not come. She was lost to them.

The ball, the rope, the grass, the cow's hoof—in the initial desperation of the case, everyone had more or less agreed that these were the objects depicted in the sweater pattern. There hadn't been time to argue about it. Now there was. Many theories grew up as to what they meant and where they had come from. Some were even close to the truth.

People speculated about a lost, invisible island, close by. People there must live as they did—enough that they went fishing at least, and wore heavy woollen sweaters against the cold at sea. And they farmed sheep. Whatever plague it had been that afflicted Inis Mór, they, the wily islanders, had managed to avert it by masquerading as those other islanders, the lost ones, who were somehow immune. This at least explained the facts. Or perhaps, the more cautious ones pointed out, crossing themselves, those unknown others had extended their protection over them. After all, they had permitted strangers to wear a pattern that was theirs, perhaps one that was intimately theirs—one that claimed the dwellers on Inis Mór as fellow islanders, parishioners, even family?

Speculation ran endlessly on the meaning of the sweater motifs. Many old women found themselves consulted and, unusually, listened to. Cables as fishermen's rope. That seemed fairly certain. Grass in patches, fields. That was common. No final consensus was ever reached on the others. What did those shapes say about the lost islanders?

The ball. Is it a ball? The round form. The sun. The sun on the fields which makes grass for cows—the cow's hoof is the other form. It's got to be. The rope, then? Have you ever heard of a dairyman who used no rope? They are farmers, like us.

The ball. It's a buoy, a spinner, a lead weight. The rope belongs to a fisherman. The form with the two triangles, it's a knot. Not a hoof. That other form was never grass. It's waves. Waves on the sea. They are fishermen, like us.

Or. The ball is the world. The rope pulls the world. The cow attached to the rope pulls it. We are the cow. We pull the world. The cow eats the grass. We are the grass. The cow eats us. In the cow, we pull the world. We eat the cow. In us, the cow pulls the world.

The ball, the rope, the grass, the cow's hoof: the cow's hoof, the grass, the rope, the ball.

About the Author

Scott Straker

SARAH TOLMIE is a poet, speculative fiction writer, and professor of English at the University of Waterloo. Her books of poetry, *Trio* in 2015 and *The Art of Dying* in 2018, both with McGill-Queen's University Press, were short-listed for the Pat Lowther Award and the Griffin Prize, respectively. Her fiction, published with Aqueduct Press, includes the novels *The Little Animals* (2019) and *The Stone Boatmen* (2014), which was a finalist for the Crawford Award, the dual novella collection *Two Travelers* (2016), and the short fiction collection *NoFood* (2014). Her poem "Ursula Le Guin in the Underworld" won the 2019 Aurora Award and the 2019 Rhysling Award.

TOR·COM

Science fiction. Fantasy. The universe.

And related subjects.

*

More than just a publisher's website, *Tor.com*

is a venue for **original fiction, comics,** and

discussion of the entire field of SF and fantasy,

in all media and from all sources. Visit our site

today — and join the conversation yourself.

9 781250 769848